THE RODRIGUEZ AFFAIR

Harry Banner turned up in London one evening in November. He had just got back from Venezuela and he wanted to see Cade. Robert Cade had known Banner six years earlier in Buenos Aires. Now Banner wanted Cade to do something for him. It was only a small favour: just to keep a parcel until he called back for it. The trouble was that Banner never did call back, because next morning he was found in his hotel room with a stab wound in his chest, dead as could be.

Some other people came for the parcel while Cade was away from his flat, but by that time he had decided also that a trip to Venezuela might throw some light on the reasons for Harry Banner's death. But in San Borja the climate could be very unhealthy for someone who went round asking too many questions.

THE RODRIGUEZ AFFAIR

James Pattinson

ROBERT HALE · LONDON

ISBN-10: 0-7090-8179-0
ISBN-13: 978-0-7090-8179-1

Robert Hale Limited
Clerkenwell House
Clerkenwell Green
London EC1R 0HT

2 4 6 8 10 9 7 5 3

Printed and bound in Great Britain by
Biddles Limited, King's Lynn

CONTENTS

ONE

SENTIMENTAL VALUE

THE TELEPHONE began to ring immediately Cade opened the door of his flat; it was as though the turning of the key in the lock had been a trigger setting it off. Cade switched on the light, crossed to the table where the instrument stood and picked up the receiver.

"Robert Cade speaking."

"So you got in at last. This is the third time I've called you." The tone was faintly aggrieved but there was a trace of relief in it too. It was a man's voice and it touched a chord in Cade's memory, though for the moment he failed to place it. "You know who this is, don't you, Bob?"

He got it then; he ought to have known at once, but the telephone distorted sounds. "Harry! Where are you? Where've you sprung from?"

"I'm in a call-box. The other answer can wait. Is it okay if I come round?"

"Of course it's okay. How long will it take you to get here?"

"Half an hour maybe."

" I'll be waiting for you. It must be five years."

" Six."

" Too long."

" Well, I'll be seeing you."

Cade heard the click as Harry rang off. He put his own telephone back on the cradle and stood for a moment or two with his fingers resting lightly on it. Of all the people he might have expected to call him that evening Harry Banner had certainly not been one. In fact he had given Banner scarcely more than a passing thought for years; he had had other things to think about.

And yet there had been a time when they had seen plenty of one another, had been pretty close friends in fact. That had been when they had both been working in Buenos Aires. He had been a bit younger in those days, still in his twenties. Now he was thirty-two and Harry would be pressing forty. It hardly seemed possible, but that was the way the years slipped past.

He took off his coat and hung it in the recess by the door. Outside it was a cheerless early November evening, but the flat was comfortably warm. He went through the sitting-room into the small kitchen, foraged in a cupboard and came up with a bottle of whisky and two glasses. He carried the bottle and the glasses back into the sitting-room and put them on a side-table.

Harry Banner! It would be good to see him again. What had he been doing with himself since those days in B.A.? Well, he would soon have the answer to that question; there would be plenty of time for talking and plenty to talk about.

Cade sat down in an armchair, picked up an evening paper, started to read. But only part of his attention was

on the print; he kept remembering that hint of relief
in Banner's voice, slight but unmistakable, as if making
contact with Cade had more to it than the mere reunion
with an old friend. So was he in trouble? Was he coming
for help, for a hand-out maybe? Well, if so, that was all
right; Banner was welcome to all the help that Cade
could give him. Cade had not forgotten that but for
Banner he might not have been alive; that kind of thing
you did not easily forget.

Banner had been right in his calculation : he arrived
just within the half-hour. Cade went to the door scarcely
knowing what to expect; he would not have been surprised to see a down-at-heel character in a threadbare
suit and frayed shirt. And he did not want it to be like
that; he did not want to see Harry Banner down on his
luck and forced to come begging for help. But he need
not have worried on that score; the man who had rung
the bell was wearing an overcoat that looked almost new,
and what was visible of the suit beneath it looked good
too. His shoes must have cost all of seven guineas.

"Bob Cade," Banner said. "By God it's good to see
you."

"And you, Harry. And you. Come in."

He closed the door and took Banner's coat and hung
it with his own; and as he did so he was thinking how
much Banner had aged, much more than the five or six
years that had passed. His hair was receding and there
were flecks of grey in the black. He was thinner too; in
the old days he had turned the scales at around fourteen
stone; now Cade would have been surprised if he could
have made more than thirteen, and he stooped a little too.

But it was in the face that marked changes had taken place; the skin was a maze of tiny wrinkles, an old man's skin.

Banner seemed to guess what was passing in Cade's mind. " You needn't tell me. I'm not as young as I was."

" We're none of us as young as we were, Harry."

" But you don't look much older, and I mean that." He stood back and sized Cade up with his eyes. The eyes had a tired look about them, a kind of world-weariness that they had not had before. " You've kept yourself trim. What do you weigh? Twelve stone?"

" About that," Cade admitted. The weight never varied much; he was pretty solidly built for his height, big-boned, plenty of muscle.

" And you always were a handsome boy," Banner said. He gave a quirky grin. " What's known as the clean-cut type. You should have been in films, making the women go weak at the knees and raking in the dough."

" Let's cut out the compliments, shall we?"

" If it embarrasses you." Banner glanced round the room; it had a wholly male look about it. " Not married?"

" Not any more."

" You were, huh?"

" Three years. It fell apart."

" Any scars?"

" No scars," Cade said.

" What are you doing these days?"

" Free-lancing. Working on a novel. This and that."

" Making money?"

" Not enough."

" Who is, boy, who is?"

Cade picked up the bottle. " Sit down. You still take this stuff?"

Banner sat down. " When it's offered."

Cade poured two glasses. " Water? I'm out of soda, I'm afraid."

" Don't contaminate it."

Cade handed him one of the glasses, took the other for himself and sat down facing Banner.

" Tell me all about it."

" All about six years? We haven't got the time."

" What's the hurry?"

" No hurry," Banner said. He spoke lightly but Cade had the impression that he was not altogether at ease, not relaxed. He wondered why.

" I had no idea you were in London, Harry."

" Arrived today."

" Where from?"

" Venezuela."

" You've been getting around."

Banner took a drink of whisky. " You know me. One of the restless type."

Sure he knew Harry Banner. That time in Buenos Aires had probably been his longest stay in one place. He had been working for a man named Oviedo, a rich man with a big estancia out on the pampas and thousands of head of cattle. Banner had been a favourite of Oviedo's and had introduced Cade to him. Oviedo, a big, open-handed, hospitable man, had invited them to the estancia and they had gone out there pretty often. They had ridden with the gauchos, learning the gauchos' skills, sleeping beside camp-fires under the stars. Great times.

Cade had never been able to discover precisely what kind of work Banner had been doing for Oviedo in Buenos Aires, and anyway it had ended abruptly with Banner pulling up stakes and moving on to some other part of the world. Cade had never known whether Oviedo had given Banner the push or whether Banner had simply decided that he had had enough of Argentina and this was the time to be moving on. Either way, the result was the same.

A few months later Cade had also left Buenos Aires. He had been working on an English·language newspaper, but the paper had folded and the staff had become redundant. Cade had decided to try his luck back in England.

" How did you find where I was living, Harry?"

" I guessed it would be London and I looked in the book. There you were."

" I might still have been in B.A."

" Could have been. But I knew that paper hit the gravel. I reckoned you'd pull out. Anyway, if you hadn't been here, that would just have been that."

Banner drained his glass. Cade refilled it.

" What were you doing in Venezuela?"

" Ever heard of a town called San Borja?"

Cade shook his head.

" Not many people have. Why should they? It's one hell of a dump way back in the interior."

" And that's where you've been?"

" Some of the time."

" Doing what?"

" Working."

" Who for?"

Banner grinned. "For a writer that's pretty lousy grammar. But I'll let it pass. I was working for a character named Gomara."

"Doing what?"

"He's got an estate of sorts some ten miles out of San Borja. I was a kind of major-domo, man about the the place."

Cade knew that Banner had not told everything. There had to be some very good reason why he would go into the heart of Venezuela to work for this man Gomara.

"What took you there?"

Banner drank some more whisky. "It's a long story. Maybe I'll tell you some day."

"But not now?"

"Not now."

Banner switched to the old days in Buenos Aires. "We had some good times, Bob."

"The best."

"Always the best times when you're young."

Neither of them spoke of that incident on the pampas, the day when Banner had saved Cade's life; but it was in Cade's mind and possibly in Banner's too. They had been rounding up a herd of cattle with Oviedo's gauchos and a thunderstorm had blown up. The herd had stampeded and Cade had been thrown from his horse. If Banner had not ridden in and taken him up on his own horse it would have been curtains for Robert Cade, no doubt about it. Banner had always played the rescue down, making light of it, but it was one reason why he had only to ask for Cade's help, anytime, anywhere, and he would get it without question. They both knew that.

Not that Cade would not have helped Banner anyway; their friendship had been enough to ensure that; but the incident on the pampas had set the seal on the contract as it were.

At this moment, however, Banner did not appear to be in need of any help, at least not of the financial kind; he looked prosperous enough. Nevertheless, there had been that hint of relief in his voice when Cade answered the phone, and it had seemed to indicate rather more than natural satisfaction at having succeeded in making contact with an old friend. There was too that suggestion of uneasiness, as though something were troubling him; sometimes his attention would wander and he would break off in mid-sentence, his mind obviously on other matters.

Finally Cade said : " What's bothering you, Harry?"

Banner looked startled. " Bothering me?"

" You've got something on your mind. Like to tell me?"

Banner shook his head. " Nothing to tell. You're imagining things." He gave his quirky grin again, but his eyes were worried. " You know me, boy; never any problems."

" All right," Cade said, " if you don't want to tell me. Maybe it's part of that long story." He noticed that Banner's glass was empty again. " Have another drink."

Banner left soon after ten. Cade offered to ring up for a taxi to take him back to his hotel, but he refused.

" Don't bother. I can manage."

" It wouldn't be any bother. Better still, why not move in here while you're in London? There's a spare room."

Banner would not hear of it. " I'm not parking myself on you. I'll be all right where I am."

" Where are you staying?"

" Not the Savoy, but it's good enough for me. I never was a luxury hound." He was side-stepping the question, avoiding a direct answer. Cade did not press him; if he wanted to keep his quarters a secret he was entitled to do so.

" Not too rough, I hope."

Banner just grinned. He was almost at the door when he turned and pulled a small flat parcel from his jacket pocket. It was wrapped in brown paper and sealed with adhesive tape; it measured about nine inches by five.

" Oh," he said, " I nearly forgot. I wonder if you'd mind hanging on to this for me for a day or two."

It seemed like something that had just come into his mind, something of no great importance; but Cade was certain that that was not so. He had a shrewd suspicion that Banner had been thinking about the parcel for most of the evening.

He took the parcel. " What is it?"

Banner looked a shade embarrassed. " Do you mind if I don't tell you that?"

" It's up to you."

" I'll tell you some other time."

" Something else for that long story?"

" Maybe."

" If it's valuable don't you think it would be better in a bank? I haven't got a safe."

Banner gave him a quick glance. " Who said it was valuable?"

" Isn't it?"

Banner hesitated for a moment; then he said : " Let's just say it has considerable sentimental value. Okay?"

" Okay. Do you want a receipt?"

" When did I ever want a receipt from you, boy?"

He moved again towards the door, then stopped again. " I may be out of town for a few days. I'll get in touch as soon as I get back. If anything happens to me—"

" You're expecting something to happen?"

" Not expecting," Banner said. " No, not expecting anything. But there's always the possibility of an accident. People get killed on the roads every day."

" But that wasn't really what you meant, was it?"

" No," Banner admitted. " It wasn't."

" Look," Cade said, " why don't you tell me what this is all about? Maybe I could help."

Banner gave a laugh and slapped him on the shoulder. " It's not about anything, Bob. Forget it."

" And the parcel—if you should have an accident?"

" Forget that too. There'll be no accident."

Cade went down with him to the street. It was a wretched night, raw and cold, with a thin drizzle falling. Banner turned up the collar of his coat.

" Still the same old filthy English weather."

" You didn't have to come back to it."

" Maybe I did," Banner said. " Maybe I did at that."

Cade watched him walking away in the yellow glow of the sodium lamps. There were a lot of cars slipping past, each one a possible lethal weapon. It was true, what Banner had said : there was always the possibility of an accident. But nobody worried his head about accidents that might happen; it was the carefully planned incident that one needed to be wary of. The question was, did Banner suspect that someone was planning just such an accident for him? And the answer to that was probably that he did, and that probably it was in some way connected with the parcel that he had left in Cade's hands. Which meant that Cade had become involved. It meant that he had become involved in some affair which he knew nothing about.

He did not much care for that kind of situation.

When he got back to the flat he examined the parcel. He felt a strong inclination to open it and take a look at the contents. Banner had not specifically forbidden him to do so, but he had almost certainly taken it for granted that Cade would not. And unfortunately the parcel was so well sealed that it would have been impossible to open it and then re-wrap it without leaving obvious evidence of the operation. Reluctantly Cade decided to let his curiosity go unsatisfied.

He glanced round the room, searching for a place in which to hide the parcel. As he had told Banner, he had no safe; but Banner had not seemed worried by the fact and had said nothing about locking the parcel away. So perhaps after all it was of no great value except from the sentimental point of view. He still did not think this was likely, because Harry Banner had always struck him as being about the most unsentimental character going; but it was not impossible. So let it go at that.

After considering various alternatives he decided to stow the parcel behind the three volumes of Prescott's " History of the Conquest of Mexico " in his bookcase. It was no real hiding-place of course, but nowhere in the flat was there any repository that would have baffled a resolute searcher for more than a few minutes at the most. And why should there be a resolute searcher anyway?

Let Prescott shoulder the responsibility.

TWO

NOT THE SAVOY

CADE WOKE to the sound of the door buzzer. He rubbed the sleep out of his eyes and switched on the light. He glanced at the bedside clock and saw that it was not yet eight. Who could be calling at that hour? Only one possible early morning visitor came into his mind and that was Harry Banner. But he had said that he was leaving town.

The buzzer continued its sleep-destroying noise; whoever was outside there pressing the button was certainly persistent.

" All right, all right," Cade muttered. " I'm coming, damn you."

He rolled out of bed, stepped into a pair of slippers and pulled on a dressing-gown. The buzzer was still going when he opened the door of the flat. A young police-constable in a peaked cap was standing outside.

The constable took his finger off the button and said : " Mr. Cade?"

" Yes," Cade said.

" Sorry to get you out of bed, sir." There was a hint

of reproach in the constable's apology, as though in fact he felt that no one had any right to be in bed at that hour. " I wonder if you'd mind getting dressed and coming with me?"

" Where to? And why?"

" There's been an incident." The constable seemed to be speaking with some delicacy. He had a round, baby-ish face and looked about eighteen. His appearance was probably deceptive. " The superintendent thinks you may be able to help him."

Cade did not like the sound of things. That bit about helping the superintendent had an ominous ring to it.

" What's this all about?" he asked. " How on earth can I help?"

" The superintendent will tell you, sir."

" And suppose I refuse to come?"

" It's up to you, sir, of course, but your co-operation would be very much appreciated."

Cade detected the carefully veiled pressure. It would be prudent to co-operate; hindering the police in the performance of their duty was not the kind of activity calculated to do you much good. Besides, his curiosity had been aroused and he was enough of a journalist not to allow curiosity to go unsatisfied if he could help it.

" You'd better come inside," he said. " I'll dress at once."

The constable walked in and closed the door behind him. Cade went to the bathroom, cleaned the stubble from his face with an electric razor, brushed his teeth and washed. He returned to the bedroom and dressed quickly. When he went back to the sitting-room he found the constable by the bookcase apparently reading the titles of the books. He wondered whether the young man had noticed that there was a parcel behind the volumes of Prescott.

" Interested in literature?" Cade asked.

" I read when I have the time," the constable said. He did not mention the parcel. There was no reason why he should, even if he had noticed it. And there was no reason to believe that he had noticed it. " Are you ready, sir?"

" There wouldn't be time for a cup of coffee first, I suppose?"

" The superintendent is inclined to be impatient. He's probably chewing his nails as it is."

" All right," Cade said. " You go ahead. I'll follow."

The constable went to the door, opened it and stepped outside. Cade took the parcel from the bookcase and slipped it into his pocket. He put on his coat and went out of the flat, locking the door behind him.

The patrol car was standing on the kerb. There was another constable sitting behind the wheel. The one who had invited Cade to go with them opened the rear door. Cade got in. The constable closed the door and got in beside the driver. The car moved off. It was the way they took villains for questioning. Cade began to feel like a villain.

" How far is it to the police-station?" he asked.

" We're not going to the station," the baby-faced constable said. " We're going to a hotel."

So it was something to do with Harry Banner. He had guessed so from the start; the mention of the hotel merely confirmed the suspicion. He wondered what trouble Harry had got himself into now, but he knew it was of no use asking the policemen he would just have to be patient for a while; all would soon be clear, and maybe he would not like it any better when it was.

It was certainly not the Savoy. It was a seedy, run-down sort of place where you might have expected to meet seedy, run-down commercial travellers or unsuccessful actors. There were half a dozen worn stone steps leading up to the front door with rust-pitted railings on each side. The door was a sickly yellow and the paint was peeling; the building itself was crushed between two other establishments in a similar line of business and of a similar seediness. In the street were two or three police cars and an ambulance, and there were several idlers hanging about and looking as if they would have liked to climb the steps and poke their inquisitive noses in at the hotel doorway but were deterred from doing so by the presence of a large uniformed policeman stationed at the entrance.

The baby-faced constable opened the car door for Cade and waited for him to step out. As Cade did so he was aware of a ripple of interest in the party of onlookers. He might have felt flattered by this evident interest in him if he had not been reasonably certain that he was being regarded as some kind of criminal who would undoubtedly soon be reaping the just reward for his misdeeds.

" This way," the constable said, and he led the way up the steps, through the doorway and into a narrow entrance hall that was more a passage than a lobby.

There was a kind of hatch opening into a cramped little office on the right, and straight ahead was a steep flight of stairs with a worn carpet and banisters that looked as though they had taken more polish from the hands of the hotel guests than from any other source. A smell of coffee and fried bacon was in the air, mingling with other, less easily definable odours that might have emanated from damp walls and inefficient plumbing.

A man was inside the cramped office. He poked his head out when Cade and the young constable came into the hotel. He had a long, sad face and pouches under his eyes, lank, thinning hair and little pits in the end of his nose like the indentations in a strawberry.

" Oh, my God !" he said. " More of you."

" I've been here before, Mr. Solly," the constable said. " You've seen me."

" Oh, my God !" Mr. Solly said. " So you have." He seemed to derive no consolation from the fact. " My God," he said, " why did this have to happen to me? As if I didn't have enough troubles already. What sort of reputation do you think this is going to give the hotel?"

Cade gathered that he was the proprietor. Judging by what he had seen of the hotel, he doubted whether anything that had happened in it could have any serious effect on its reputation; but perhaps Mr. Solly saw qualities in it that were invisible to the normal eye.

" Oh, my God !" he said. " This is going to ruin me."

" I doubt it," the young constable said, and he began to climb the stairs.

Cade followed him.

The room was on the second floor. It was not large

and it seemed to be full of men. The furniture was Spartan; it consisted of a single bed, a wooden wardrobe, a dressing-table and a chair. Across from the door was a window; the wallpaper had a pattern of flowers, rather faded, as though autumn had come to them also.

The young constable approached one of the men and spoke to him with some deference. "Mr. Cade, sir."

"Thank you, Sims," the man said. He did not look as though he had been chewing his nails; he looked splendidly calm. "That will be all at the moment."

The constable withdrew from the room. Cade could hear him walking down the corridor towards the stairs.

"Good of you to come so quickly, Mr. Cade. My name's Alletson. Detective superintendent." He was a heavily-built man with a pale, squarish face and blue eyes. "Rather nasty business here, I'm afraid." He sounded mildly regretful; his voice was a trifle hoarse and as he spoke he rubbed two fingers up and down his left cheek as though testing the smoothness of his morning shave.

Cade noticed that all except one of the men in the room were standing. One was using a camera and lighting surroundings with the momentary glare of flash-bulbs, another had a small brush and a small jar of some kind of powder, a third appeared to be taking measurements. The odd man out was lying on the floor. He was not moving. He was lying on his left side and he had his back to Cade, so that it was impossible to see his face completely. But Cade did not need to see the face to know that the man was Harry Banner; he recognised the suit and he knew Banner's shape. He knew too that Banner was dead.

" I'd like you to tell me whether you can identify this man," Alletson said.

He put a hand on Cade's arm and guided him as he might have guided a blind person to the other side of the man on the floor.

Cade looked down at Banner and felt a hot wave of anger. There was linoleum on the floor, and Banner's cheek was on the linoleum and his eyes were open. But they were not seeing anything; they would never see anything again. His jacket was unbuttoned and his shirt was visible. There was a dark stain on the shirt and there was a patch of something dark on the linoleum also; but he had not bled much.

" You know who this man is?" Alletson asked.

" Yes," Cade said. " It's Harry Banner."

He was still looking at Banner's face and remembering things; remembering Buenos Aires and the pampas and the great times they had had; remembering above all what a good friend Harry had been. And there was a hot anger in him, burning inside him, because somebody had killed that friend and now there was nothing that anyone could do to bring him back.

Alletson was pulling at his arm again. " Come over to the window. I'd be glad if you'd answer a few questions."

The window looked out on to a car park. The light had strengthened a little, but it was obviously going to be a sunless day. There was nothing cheerful in the view from the window, nothing to raise the spirits.

" Bring the chair, sergeant," Alletson said. " For Mr. Cade."

" I don't need a chair," Cade said. He rested his hands on the window-sill, holding his anger.

" Mr. Banner was a friend of yours, Mr. Cade?"

" Yes." Cade turned and saw that the sergeant had his notebook out. The sergeant looked about thirty; he had a long chin and sunken cheeks; his face was expressionless.

" When did you last see him?"

" Last night. He rang up at about seven and came round to my flat. He left a little after ten."

" Any particular reason why he should come to see you?"

" We'd known each other in Buenos Aires. That was six years ago. Hadn't met since. It was natural he should want to see me. He didn't arrive back in England until yesterday."

" I know," Alletson said.

Cade accepted the statement without surprise. The police had been there long enough to have gone through Banner's things; they would have found his passport and any other papers he might have had about him. If the parcel had been there they would have found that too. Cade knew that he ought to tell Alletson about the parcel, but he said nothing.

" What did Mr. Banner talk about?" Alletson asked.

" About the old days; things we'd done. You know how it is when friends meet after a long time."

" Did he tell you what he'd been doing lately?"

" He said he'd been working for a man named Gomara in Venezuela."

" Doing what?"

" He didn't say exactly. He seemed a bit reticent about himself in that respect."

" Had you kept in touch with him since you last saw

him in Buenos Aires?"

" No. I didn't even know whether he was alive until he rang up yesterday."

" He didn't mention any trouble that he might have been involved in?"

" Trouble?"

" Any enemies he'd made?"

" No. As far as I knew he had no enemies."

Alletson pursed his lips. " It seems that he had nevertheless."

" Yes," Cade said. And then : " How did you get my name and address?"

" He'd jotted it down in a notebook."

" He must have done that when he looked it up in the telephone directory."

" Then he tore the page out."

" Tore it out?"

" We assume so. We couldn't find it."

" Then how—"

" He must have pressed rather heavily on the pencil. The impression went through to the next page."

Cade was thinking. It could, of course, have been as Alletson had suggested; Banner could have torn out the page and destroyed it. On the other hand, it was just as possible that the murderer had taken it. And if that should be so other unpleasant possibilities came up; such as another visit to his own flat, and not this time by a police-constable.

" When was he killed?" Cade asked.

" Almost certainly soon after he returned last night. His body was discovered by a maidservant. He'd left instructions to be called early."

" Yes. He was going away for a few days."

" He told you that?"

" Yes."

" Did he say where he was going?"

" No. Just that he was going away."

" But he intended coming back?"

" Yes."

" Did he make any arrangements to meet you again?"

" Nothing definite. He said he would let me know when he was back in London."

" You knew he was staying in this hotel of course?"

" No. He didn't tell me where he was staying."

" Didn't you consider that strange?"

" I thought he had his own reasons for not telling me. I didn't press him."

" Perhaps he didn't want to involve you."

" In what?"

Alletson gave a wry smile. " If we knew that our problem would be half solved. But perhaps we shall find out. The two men might be able to help us with the answers—if we could trace them."

" What two men?"

The photographer was packing his gear. " I've finished here, sir."

Alletson nodded. The fingerprint man also appeared to have run out of likely material for his attentions.

" What two men?" Cade repeated.

Alletson looked at him. " Didn't I tell you? The proprietor saw Banner arrive last night at about a quarter to eleven with two men. They were walking close together. They went up the stairs together."

" Would he recognise them again?"

" He doesn't think so. They had their coat collars turned up and hats pulled down low over their faces."

" Did he see them go away?"

" He caught a glimpse of two men leaving the hotel about half an hour later. Just the back view as they went out of the door. He believes it was the same two men."

" So they were the men who killed Harry Banner?"

" We don't know that," Alletson said.

" It seems pretty obvious."

" In my business we try to avoid jumping to the obvious conclusion. It isn't always the right one."

" Didn't anybody hear any noise coming from this room? A struggle or something of that kind."

" Nothing unusual. Besides, killing a man with a knife can be quite a silent operation—when it is done by an expert. Whoever killed Mr. Banner was certainly an expert."

" What makes you think that?"

" There was only one thrust. It was enough."

" Have you found the knife?"

Alletson shook his head sadly. " Unfortunately, no."

Cade looked again out of the window. The view had become no less depressing. The day seemed to be trying to make up its mind whether to be rainy or merely grey and cold. When he turned his gaze back to the room he saw that two ambulancemen had come in with a stretcher.

" All right," Alletson said. " You can take him away now."

They lifted Banner on to the stretcher and draped a blanket over him. They had a little difficulty in getting their burden out of the room; the corridor was narrow and they had to tilt the stretcher. Cade felt an urge to shout at them, warning them to be careful because it was his friend Harry Banner that they were carrying, but he said nothing. They managed to get out of the room without mishap.

"Did Mr. Banner say anything about being followed from Venezuela?" Alletson asked.

Cade glanced at him in surprise. "Why should he have been followed?"

"I don't know why. But it seems probable that he was."

"I don't see it."

"He'd hardly been back in this country long enough to make enemies."

"What makes you think he was killed by enemies? The motive could have been simple robbery."

"His wallet was still in his pocket. There was money in it. Does that look like simple robbery to you?"

Cade was silent.

Alletson was regarding him keenly. "They could, of course, have been looking for something else, something more valuable perhaps. I suppose you couldn't make any suggestion as to what that something else might have been?"

"No," Cade said. "I couldn't."

"This going away that he proposed—you don't think it was to avoid someone? You don't think he might have been going into hiding for a time?"

"It's a possibility," Cade admitted. "But from what I remember of Harry in the old days, he was not the kind of man to be easily scared."

"Nor a man to give away information under pressure?"

"It would be like opening a clam."

Alletson drummed with his fingers on the window-sill. "I wonder whether they got what they came for?"

"That's anybody's guess," Cade said.

Alletson nodded. "Yes," he said slowly, "I suppose it is."

Cade made his own way back to the flat. Alletson had offered him transport but he had refused.

"I think I'll take a walk. I could do with some fresh air to clear my head."

"If you think of anything that might help while you're walking, let me know."

"Like what?"

"You tell me, Mr. Cade. Here's the phone number."

Cade's flat was on the third floor of a red-brick building that had been erected in the 1930s. The lift was having one of its frequent spells out of order and he had to go up by the stairs. He let himself in with his key and closed the door behind him, and he knew at once that he had had visitors. The odour of cigar smoke told him so. He never smoked cigars.

They had made a thorough search, and if the parcel had been there they would undoubtedly have found it. Cade guessed that they had kept watch on the flat and had waited until he had left in the police car before breaking in. The lock on the door was the kind that could be forced with a strip of celluloid; it would not have bothered them much.

Cade was glad that he had had the foresight to take

the parcel with him. Prescott would not have protected it; Prescott was lying on the floor with a lot of other books. Cade did not think the visitors had been reading about the Conquest of Mexico.

He decided that the time had come to find out just what it was that Harry Banner had died for. He pulled the parcel out of his pocket, picked up a pair of scissors and cut the wrapping. Under the wrapping was a small wooden box that had once contained cigars. There were no cigars in it now; instead there was a small chamois leather bag fastened with a string. In the bag were a number of very fine diamonds.

THREE

TAIL

CADE LOOKED at the diamonds and wondered just how Banner had managed to get them into the country. It was a question that was never likely to be answered now and it was not really important anyway. The important fact was that he had done so. And much good it had done him.

But there were other questions that needed answers. How, for example, had Banner got possession of the diamonds in the first place, and had he had any right to them? And the men who had killed him—had they any right to them either? One thing was certain about those characters: they were prepared to go to a considerable amount of trouble to gain, or regain, possession of them. Which was not altogether surprising, for they were large stones, and there were, as he discovered when he counted them, no fewer than twenty. It was a nice round number, very, very nice indeed.

He picked up one of the diamonds and weighed it in his hand. He was not an expert on precious stones, but he knew enough to realise that this little lot was almost certainly worth several thousands of pounds.

" Well, well, well," he muttered. " Sentimental value, eh, Harry?" A lot of people could get sentimental about things of that description.

In fact, when he came to think about it, he was not altogether devoid of sentimentality himself.

He put the diamonds back in the chamois leather bag, tied the string and dropped the bag into his jacket pocket.

After that he rang up the police and reported that his flat had been broken into.

Detective Superintendent Alletson himself came along.

" You took your time about letting us know," he said. It sounded like an accusation.

" I didn't come straight back," Cade said.

Alletson grunted; he did not look particularly pleased with life. He might have looked less pleased if he had known that Cade was withholding information.

" Anything missing?"

" As far as I can tell, nothing at all."

" You wouldn't have any idea about what the intruders were looking for, I suppose?"

" It's anybody's guess."

" I'm asking you to guess," Alletson said.

" I haven't a clue."

Alletson winced. " I never did care for that expression. Do you think this business could have had any connection with that visit Mr. Banner paid you yesterday evening?"

" I don't see how it could."

" Well, put it this way. Suppose those two men who

went to the hotel with Banner last night couldn't find what they were looking for in his room, and suppose they found your address in his notebook and decided maybe he'd left what they wanted in your keeping. Then suppose they waited until you were out of the way and then gave this place a going-over. How does that sound to you?"

"It's an interesting theory," Cade said. Alletson was certainly no fool. Which was not really surprising, since he would hardly have reached his present rank in the C.I.D. if he had been.

"But you still can't suggest what the object of the search was?"

"No," Cade said.

Alletson grunted again; the grunt managed to convey a certain amount of disbelief. He looked at the bookcase. The three volumes of Prescott were still lying on the floor where the intruders had thrown them.

"It must have been something that could have been hidden in a bookcase; otherwise they would not have pulled out the books."

"Plenty of things could be hidden in a bookcase."

Alletson regarded him with a certain amount of disapproval. "You're not being very helpful, are you?"

"I'm doing my best," Cade said.

"God keep me from your worst."

"Have you found those two men?"

"This is London. It's a big city."

"I suppose you've checked with the airlines, that sort of thing? People coming in from Venezuela."

Alletson gave him a sour look. "Are you trying to teach me my business, Mr. Cade?"

Cade gathered that Alletson had checked. He also gathered that if Alletson had picked up any information he was not going to hand it round to all and sundry.

"By the way," Cade said, "I'm thinking of taking a trip down to Venezuela myself."

Alletson's chin jerked up. "For what purpose?"

"I'm a journalist. I might pick up a story."

"You wouldn't be thinking of carrying out some kind of private investigation, would you?"

"What makes you think I should wish to do that?"

"Some people always think they can do better than the police. Fancy themselves a lot of little Sherlock Holmses."

"I don't even fancy myself a little Sexton Blake."

"Frankly, I'd rather you didn't go just yet," Alletson said. "I may need you here."

"Are you telling me I'm not to leave the country?"

"I'm not in a position to stop you if you really insist on going." Alletson seemed to be breathing a trifle hard. "I'm just saying I'd rather you postponed your trip for a while, that's all."

"Don't worry," Cade said. "I'll be back in time for the trial. You haven't caught your men yet."

"I am perfectly aware of that," Alletson said. And he looked rather savage about it.

When Alletson and his assistant had departed Cade put on his coat and left the flat. A man was standing in the entrance to the building; he was wearing a black raincoat and a felt hat; he was thick-set and slightly less than average height and he had a dark, pock-marked face and high cheekbones.

Cade could not help noticing him because he was so obviously trying to give the impression that he was completely uninterested in Cade. As Cade went past he pulled a small cigar from his pocket and lit it with a match.

Cade had walked about thirty paces down the street when he glanced back and saw the man with the cigar also leave the building. He hesitated a moment at the pavement as though undecided about which direction to take and glanced up at the sky. Cade turned his head to the front and walked on for another dozen paces, then glanced back again. As he had expected, the man with the cigar was following.

Cade passed two side-turnings, then crossed the street and continued on the other side. A little later the man with the cigar crossed also. It was so obvious that Cade could have laughed. Either the man was a very inexperienced tail or he took Cade for a fool.

They came to a park enclosed by iron railings. At the far end of the park was the entrance to an Underground station. Cade walked down the steps and came to the small booking-hall. He bought a ticket to Holborn and crossed to the lift which was waiting. Just as the gates closed he saw the man with the cigar hurrying down the steps into the booking-hall.

The lift stopped, the gates clashed open and Cade made his way to the platform serving the southbound trains. Only about half a dozen people were on the platform. Cade walked to the far end, then turned and waited for the man with the cigar to appear. A few seconds later he did so. He too walked towards the end of the platform, but stopped before reaching Cade. They stood about ten yards apart and waited for the train to come in, ignoring each other.

The train came out of the tunnel like a maggot pushing its way out of an apple. It stopped with a hiss of brakes and the doors opened. Cade got in first; the man with the cigar followed him in. There were very few people in the carriage and Cade sat down on the seat nearest the doors. The man with the cigar sat down on the opposite side. He had smoked the cigar half-way down and seemed to be enjoying it. He was not wearing gloves and when he lifted his hand to take the cigar out of his mouth Cade saw that he had stubby fingers and was wearing a gold signet ring. His teeth were discoloured and uneven. He was not by any reckoning a handsome man.

The train stopped at a number of stations and the seats began to fill. Cade did not move. The man with the cigar seemed to be studying the advertisements with great attention. They came to Warren Street, Goodge Street, Tottenham Court Road. Cade waited until the doors were starting to close, then jumped up from his seat and made a dive for them. He just managed to squeeze through as they slid together. The man with the cigar was a moment too late; glancing back Cade caught a glimpse of his face on the other side of the doors before the train gathered speed and carried him away.

Cade changed to the Central Line and a few minutes later was getting out at Holborn.

Holden Bales had a small workshop up two flights of carpetless stairs in an ancient building not far from Hatton Garden. The smallness and apparent dinginess

of the establishment were misleading : Holden Bales em-
ployed only four people but he had a very thriving business. From this and other such unlikely-seeming places
came those magnificent rings and bracelets and neck-
laces that might eventually adorn the rich and the
famous, royalty, film stars, singers, ballerinas, duchesses
and countesses, ambassadors' wives and the wives of
Greek shipowners; at these cramped benches splendid
jewels were fixed in equally splendid settings of gold or
platinum by men in grubby overalls who had perfected
their skills by years of apprenticeship and practice.

Holden Bales himself would never have impressed
anyone who did not know him as a person of substance.
He was a thin, round-shouldered man of about forty-five
with a large bald head fringed at the back and sides with
the unkempt remnants of sandy hair, and his nose looked
as though it had keen kept so much to the grindstone
that it had been ground to the sharpest point imaginable
in such an organ. He always bought cheap ready-made
suits and wore them until they almost dropped off him,
and quite frequently he forgot to shave for two or three
days on end. Added to this, he was known and respected
by everyone of any importance in the London jewellery
trade and he also happened to be Robert Cade's
cousin.

Cade mounted the two flights of stairs, pushed open
a door that seemed to be hiding away in a dark corner,
and found himself in the hot, close workshop with its
characteristic and undefinable odour and its suggestion
of a medieval alchemist's laboratory. Bales was standing
by one of the benches apparently conferring with a grey-
haired man on the subject of some design for a tiara,

but when Cade entered he left the bench and came to greet him.

"Bob, my boy! This is an unexpected pleasure. Haven't seen you for months. What have you been doing with yourself? Keeping your nose clean, I hope."

"You bet I have," Cade said.

"Good, good. Ethel will be glad to hear that. She worries about you, Bob, she really does."

He seemed genuinely pleased to see his cousin, and Cade felt a little guilty because he had a standing invitation to go down to Holden's place in Surrey and very seldom did so. Ethel, Holden's wife, was the fly in the ointment; she was a large, domineering woman who always lectured him on his moral duty as a writer or some such nonsense. Moreover, she was about the worst cook he had ever had the misfortune to encounter. One day poor old Holden would drop dead from heartburn and that would be just one more life sacrificed on the altar of the domestic dining-table.

"Tell her not to worry," Cade said. And then: "I want your help, Holden."

Bales's face took on an expression of deep concern. "So you are in trouble. Well, if it's financial you know you can count on me. But don't mention it to Ethel."

"Thanks, Holden; I appreciate the offer, but I don't need money. It's something rather different. Look, can we talk in private?"

"Come into my office."

The office was a room not much bigger than a fair-sized cupboard with grimy windows which seemed more intent on keeping light out than on letting it in. There were a couple of hard chairs and a table, a steel filing cabinet, a safe, and a clutter of ledgers and loose papers.

Bales closed the door and said : " Well, what is it then?"

" This," Cade said. He pulled the chamois leather bag from his pocket and tipped the contents out on to the table.

Holden Bales made a faint hissing noise through pursed lips. " You have been busy. Where, in heaven's name, did you collect those?"

" Shall we skip that question for the moment?" Cade suggested. " What I really want you to do is give me some idèa of what those stones are worth."

Bales said nothing. He took a magnifying glass from his pocket and screwed it into his eye. With the aid of this he examined each stone in turn. Then he took them to a balance and weighed them. He made some calculations with the help of a pencil and a sheet of paper, hummed a snatch of *La donna e mobile* and finally treated Cade to a long hard stare.

" Well?" Cade said. " How much?"

" In round figures—one hundred and forty thousand pounds."

Cade whistled. " As much as that?"

" Certainly not less."

" That's a lot of little potatoes."

" It's a lot of money too," Bales said.

Cade looked at the diamonds and then at Bales. " Now, Holden, I'm going to ask you to do something else for me."

" Is it within the law?"

" Oh, I should think so."

" You don't sound very certain."

" I'm not a lawyer."

" Well, fire away," Bales said. " Let me hear the worst."

" I want you to keep these stones for me for a while."

Bales frowned slightly. He did not look at all happy. " Before I agree to that I think you ought to tell me something about them. How they came into your possession, where they came from, that sort of thing."

" They were left with me by a friend," Cade said.

" And the friend?"

" He died."

" Unfortunate," Bales said. " Did the stones legally belong to him?"

" I've no reason to believe they didn't."

" Did he tell you they did?"

" He didn't tell me anything about them."

Bales still looked worried. " It all sounds highly irregular. Why do you want me to keep them?"

" I'm leaving shortly for Venezuela."

" For how long?"

" A few weeks maybe. I'm not sure. Depends on events."

" Has your journey anything to do with these?"

" Could have—in a way."

Bales hesitated.

" You don't need to worry," Cade said. " You won't be involved in any funny business. All you have to do is hang on to the diamonds until I come back. Then I'll take them off your hands."

Bales looked at them thoughtfully for a while; then he shrugged. " All right, Bob. It's against my better judgement but I'll do it."

" Thanks, Holden. I knew I could depend on you."

Bales picked up the diamonds and put them back in the chamois leather bag. " I won't keep them here of course." He pulled the string tight and tied it. " I'll give you a receipt."

" I don't need a receipt from you," Cade said.

Harry Banner had not wanted a receipt either. He hoped it was not an omen.

Cade got in touch with Alletson later on the telephone.

" What's on your mind, Mr. Cade?" Alletson inquired.

" Did you put a tail on me?"

" Now why would I do a thing like that, Mr. Cade?"

" I don't know why you would. I'm asking you if you did."

" And I'm telling you I didn't," Alletson said. " What makes you think I did?"

" Somebody tailed me from my flat soon after you left. I shook him off in the Tube."

" If it had been one of my men you wouldn't have shaken him off so easily. The chances are you wouldn't even have known you were being tailed. What did this character look like?"

" Stocky build, dark-haired, sun-tanned, pockmarked. He was wearing a black raincoat and a felt hat. Had a gold signet ring on one finger and was smoking a cigar."

" I wish you'd brought him along to me," Alletson said. " It sounds like a man we'd be glad to interview."

" He didn't look like a man I'd want to interview. Not unless he had handcuffs on him."

Alletson was silent for a moment; then he said : " Are

you quite sure, Mr. Cade, that you've told me all you
know."

"That might be a tall order."

"You know what I mean." Alletson sounded snap-
pish. "All you know about this Banner business."

"Everything," Cade said.

"It's strange that a man should follow you. Strange
that your flat should be ransacked. Somebody is certainly
looking for something."

"They're looking in the wrong place."

"When do you propose leaving the country?"

"As soon as I can get an airline reservation."

"I'd still rather you stayed here for a while."

"Sorry," Cade said. "I've got my living to think
about."

"You might give a thought to your dying too while
you're at it," Alletson said, and rang off.

FOUR

THE PHOENIX

THE DAKOTA flopped down on the airfield like a tired old vulture. The airfield was hot and dusty and arid. To the east a few wispy clouds floated across the sky, high and thin as gauze. Away to the south mountains shimmered in the heat, intangible as dreams.

There were five other passengers in the Dakota besides Cade, as well as a quantity of freight. From Caracas the flight had been relatively uneventful, except that once or twice the pilot had come aft and argued fiercely with one of the passengers. It was an argument that seemed to have been going on since before the flight had begun; it could have been going on for years. The pilot was a plump young man wearing a red shirt and a baseball cap; the passenger was grey-haired, paunchy, with a voice like a crow. One of the other passengers informed Cade that the two were father and son, so perhaps the argument had been going on ever since the pilot had learnt to talk. Cade was not bothered as long as it did not take his mind off his flying duties. The pilot did not inspire Cade with much confidence, but even at that he was

better than the co-pilot. The co-pilot looked like a junkie
who was not getting his regular fix.

The Dakota bumped a little as its undercarriage hit
the runway. It slowed, came to a stop, then turned and
taxied towards the control buildings, leaving clouds of
dust eddying behind it.

Cade released his seat-belt and passed a tongue over
gummy lips. He wondered why he had come. It was
probably a fool's errand and he would find nothing. No
doubt it would have been more sensible to have taken
Superintendent Alletson's advice and to have stayed in
England; but it was a bit late to think about that
now. He was here and he might as well go through
with it.

Outside the plane the heat was oppressive. There was
a low brick building with a control tower at one end
and a wind-sock drooping from a pole. On the wall of the
building was painted in large letters : San Borja. Below
this in slightly smaller letters was the word : Aeropuerto.

It seemed to Cade a somewhat pretentious description
for such an establishment.

There were few formalities at San Borja Airport. On
the other side of the control building a rusty minibus
was waiting to take passengers into the town. They got
in. The driver started the engine and the minibus shuddered. There was a noise like steel bolts being ground in
a mill and the gears finally sorted themselves out and
they were away.

It was about a mile on a rough road. The driver
seemed to be possessed by the demon of speed and the
minibus swayed like a ship in a storm, bouncing over
rocks and potholes and sliding perilously into ruts. A

large woman sitting next to Cade was thrown heavily against him and smiled an apology.

" Such a road, señor."

" Why is it not repaired?" Cade asked.

She laughed as though he had made a joke. " In San Borja roads are never repaired. Who would pay?" She looked at Cade with some interest. " You are a stranger to San Borja, señor." It was a statement rather than a question.

" Yes," Cade said.

" You have friends here perhaps?"

" No. No friends."

" So? You come on business?" She was frankly curious. She had black, coarse hair combed back from her forehead and large, dark eyes which had a certain calculation in them. Her nose was prominent and on her upper lip there was a slight growth of hair. Her chin descended to her neck in a series of mobile curves and her ample bosom seemed only precariously contained by the cotton dress she was wearing. She was possibly between thirty-five and forty years old.

" In a way, yes," Cade admitted.

" You have arranged accommodation of course?"

" No," Cade said, " but I suppose I can find a hotel."

" In San Borja," the woman said, " there is only one good hotel—the Phoenix. I would not advise you to go anywhere else. At the Phoenix you will have a good room, good food, good service. And you will not be cheated."

She seemed, Cade thought, to be pressing the virtues of the Phoenix with considerable enthusiasm. " You would not, perhaps, have some interest in this hotel?"

" But naturally," she said. " I own it."

" Ah, I see."

" I am Señora Torres."

" I am Robert Cade."

Señora Torres nodded. " You are not, of course, Venezuelan, Señor Cade. You speak Spanish very well but with a certain accent. You are perhaps American?"

" English."

" So?"

Cade had the impression that an added flicker of interest appeared in Señora Torres's large dark eyes, as though the mention of his nationality had touched some nerve; but he could have been mistaken.

" In this country," she said, " we regard the English as our friends. We have not forgotten how many Englishmen fought beside us in our struggle for independence."

" That was a long time ago."

" Some of us have long memories," Señora Torres said.

The minibus bumped and rattled on its way and the first houses of the town appeared. They were not very impressive. Banner had described San Borja as a dump and perhaps he had not been far out in his assessment; at a first glance it did not look a very prosperous place.

After brief consideration Cade decided to try Señora Torres's hotel. She had probably exaggerated its attractions, but at least he would be saved the bother of looking for alternative accommodation. And if it did not come up to specification there was nothing to prevent him from moving.

The Phoenix faced the Plaza, an open, unpaved square in the centre of the town where some children were playing and two old men were sleeping in the shade of a tree. The Phoenix was a white, two-storied building standing by itself. It had nine large windows in the Plaza side and a door that was wide open. The minibus stopped outside the hotel and Cade and Señora Torres got out. The señora's feet had scarcely touched the ground before she began to shout in a voice that would have done credit to a town crier.

"Pancho! Pancho! Where are you, you scoundrel?"

After a few moments of this a dried-up wisp of a man appeared in the doorway and stared at Señora Torres without saying a word. He had a face like a pickled walnut and he was wearing faded blue denims and espadrilles.

"Don't stand there like an idiot," she cried. "Take Señor Cade's luggage."

Cade had a suitcase and a holdall. Pancho took them from him. He also took Señora Torres's bag.

"This way, señor," the lady said, and she led the way into the hotel like a galleon under full sail.

The floor of the lobby was tiled and it was appreciably cooler inside. On the right there was a counter of dark polished wood with a key-rack on the wall behind, and there was also a wide stairway leading to the upper floor. There was no one behind the counter; in fact no one else in sight. Señora Torres raised her voice again and sent it echoing through the hotel.

"Jorge!"

A door opened at the far end of the lobby and a man came in. He was younger than the woman and he was handsome in a swarthy, villainous kind of way. Immediately he saw Señora Torres he rushed to meet her, flung his arms round her splendid body and kissed her ardently on the mouth.

" Welcome home, Maria my love. It has been so long."

" Nonsense," Señora Torres said. " It has been only five days." She was going through the motions of being annoyed by this effusive greeting, but it was apparent that she liked it nevertheless.

" Five days !" Jorge exclaimed. " Without the light of my life, an age."

He looked and sounded, Cade thought, like a tenth rate actor in a Victorian melodrama.

Señora Torres freed herself from his enthusiastic embrace and turned to her guest. " Señor Cade, this is my husband."

Jorge Torres made a slight bow. He had a black moustache and long side-whiskers. His smile was like an advertisement for dental cream.

" So happy to meet you, señor. You intend to stay long at the Phoenix?"

" That depends on circumstances."

" We shall be enchanted to serve you for as long as you care to be with us."

Cade had a suspicion that there was a hint of mockery in Torres's eyes and in his smile. He had a feeling that Torres would as soon have seen him in hell as he would have served him.

" What rooms have we, Jorge?" Señora Torres asked, cutting off any further professions of welcome.

" The same as when you went away. No one has left; no one has arrived. All is as it was."

Señor Torres spoke to Pancho, who had been standing with the bags in his hands waiting patiently for instructions. "Take Señor Cade's luggage to Room Seven."

"Yes, señor." He went away up the stairs.

It was Jorge Torres who showed Cade to his room. "The best room in the hotel, señor." He thumped the bed. "Good mattress." He moved to the window. "And what a splendid view, is it not?"

It was in fact a view of the Plaza; but Cade had not come to admire the view from a hotel window. His purpose in coming to San Borja was to try to find out how Harry Banner had come into possession of one hundred and forty thousand pounds' worth of diamonds and, if possible, why he had been murdered and by whom.

He wondered whether it would not be a good idea to make a start by questioning Jorge Torres. He might at least know something about the Gomara estate. He was still turning the idea over in his mind when Torres himself asked a question; it was one that Señora Torres had asked earlier on the bus.

"You are American, señor?"

"No," Cade said. "I am English."

"So?"

In Señora Torres's eyes Cade had imagined a flicker of interest on learning his nationality; in her husband the interest was more obvious.

"We do not often have Englishmen in this hotel. San Borja is not, as you might say, a tourist resort. It is an honour of course."

"Not often?" Cade tried to make his tone flat, casually conversational, no more. "Then you have sometimes had Englishmen?"

" One," Torres said. " No others in my time. You know him perhaps?"

" It seems unlikely."

" And yet perhaps not impossible. His name was Banner. Harry Banner. A strange name."

Torres was watching Cade closely; it could have been that he was looking for some reaction on Cade's part to the mention of Banner's name.

Cade looked down into the Plaza. The old men were still asleep under the tree; a car went past, raising dust, the children threw stones at it in a half-hearted sort of way; they did not hit it.

" This man Banner," Cade said. " Was he a tourist?"

Torres laughed. " Are you a tourist, señor?"

" No."

" Neither was he."

Two of the children in the Plaza had started to fight. The others were urging them on; their thin voices came up to the room like the chatter of starlings.

" Was he alone?"

" No, señor, not alone. There were two other men with him."

" Englishmen?"

" No. South American."

" Did they stay long?"

" Señor Banner did not stay long. He went to work for Señor Gomara. The other two stayed."

" Señor Gomara?"

" He has an estate south of the town. Fifteen kilometres maybe. It is not a large estate. I think Señor Gomara has retired from business."

" You have seen him?"

" No one sees Señor Gomara. He never comes into town. He is, as you might say, a very retiring man in every respect." Torres smiled, teeth gleaming below the black moustache. " Perhaps he has reasons."

" What reasons?"

Torres gave a lift of the shoulders. " Who knows? There are many possible reasons why a man should not wish to be seen. If he were being hunted by the police for example."

" So you think Señor Gomara is a fugitive from justice? Is that so?"

" I did not say that. I do not know what he is. All I know is that he bought the estate six or seven years ago and that he never leaves it."

" How can you be sure he never leaves it? Do you keep watch on him?"

" This is a small town. We all know who passes through San Borja, and he could not go any other way, except to the mountains. And who would wish to go to the mountains?"

Cade stroked his chin reflectively; he had shaved early in the day and already it felt a little rough. " Those two men who came with Señor Banner—are they still here?"

Torres shook his head. " No, señor. When Señor Banner left the Gomara estate they left San Borja too."

" When did Banner leave?"

Torres made a rapid mental calculation. " I think it was maybe ten days ago. Perhaps more."

" And the other men left with him?"

" Not with him, señor; after him. I do not think Señor Banner told them he was going. When they heard he was gone they were very angry. There was not another flight to Caracas for three days."

" Three days !" Banner had had a good start on them, but they had made up the leeway. Perhaps he had been held up in Caracas or somewhere else on the way to London. But that was assuming that the two men who had accompanied Banner to his room at Mr. Solly's hotel had been the same two men who had arrived with him in San Borja. There was no proof of that, of course, but it was all Lombard Street to a china orange that it was so.

" They were very impatient," Torres said. " They tried to hire a car to take them, but even if they had been able to get one it would have taken maybe longer than three days. The roads between here and Caracas are not good. I told them so, and in the end they decided to wait for the Dakota. But oh, señor, they were very angry. I wonder what it was that Señor Banner did to annoy them ?"

Cade was wondering the same thing.

Torres was smiling again. " I think perhaps you know these men, señor."

" No," Cade said. " I don't know them."

" But you know Señor Banner perhaps?"

" Perhaps," Cade admitted. It would have been futile to deny it. He had shown too much interest and Torres was shrewd enough to see that the interest was not mere casual curiosity.

" He is a friend of yours perhaps?"

" Perhaps."

" For a friend of mine," Torres said, "I should be worried with two such angry men following him."

Cade looked again at the Plaza. One of the boys was on the ground with another sitting on him. The old men had not moved.

" Did one of these South Americans have a pock-marked face and a gold signet ring?"

" He did."

" A thick-set man?"

" Yes, señor; that is the man."

" His name?"

" He called himself Manuel Lopez."

" And the other?"

" Luis Guzman. He was taller, thin, hard-faced, with a drooping moustache and a scar on his forehead, so." Torres indicated with his finger a point on his own forehead, just above the left eyebrow.

Cade had turned away from the window. He looked steadily at Torres. " Can I trust you not to mention this conversation that we have had? To speak of it to no one?"

" You can trust me, señor."

" Good."

" Nevertheless," Torres said, " it might be easier for me to remember that you do not wish me to talk of this matter if I had some small token to stir my memory. You understand what I mean?"

" I understand," Cade said. He took out his wallet and extracted fifty bolivars. He handed the notes to Torres. " Perhaps this will serve to remind you. Please regard it as a small token."

Torres accepted the money.

The dining-room of the Phoenix Hotel was large

enough to have accommodated at least three times as many guests as appeared to be in residence. Cade had a table to himself; it was in a corner and from it he had a view of the whole room. A tall, lean man with pale yellow hair, trimmed short, was sitting at a nearby table with a woman in a blue dress. The man had that kind of hard youthful look that some men carry well into middle age with scarcely any noticeable change; he had light blue eyes and a curious habit of tapping his chin with his knuckles when making a point in conversation. He was wearing a brown lightweight suit and a rather jazzy tie.

The woman was, Cade reckoned, a little on the right side of thirty; she had raven black hair which came down to the level of her chin and then curved inward, making a kind of living frame for the oval of her face. There was a vivid brilliance about her that caught Cade's attention; when she laughed at something the man had said her laughter was soft and vibrant, a sound to make the heart beat faster; so might Helen have laughed when Paris whispered to her.

The food, rather to Cade's surprise, was excellent. It was served by a depressed-looking waiter who seemed to be doing it all under penance. He poured wine with the air of carrying out his last act on earth and he sighed gently when he put down the plates. He would have made a very good attendant at a funeral.

Señora Torres herself came to inquire whether Cade was satisfied. "It is as good as I told you it would be?"

"You were too modest, señora. It is the best."

She looked pleased. "I am glad it is to your liking. And your room also?"

"Could not be better. You need have no fear that I shall be looking for other accommodation while I remain in San Borja."

"I am happy to hear you say so," Señora Torres said. Then she lowered her voice and added: "You had a very long talk with Jorge this afternoon. I should perhaps warn you, though he is my husband, it has to be admitted that he is a very great liar. You must not believe everything that he tells you. And do not give him money; above all, señor, do not give him money."

"I will remember the warning, señora."

She smiled and moved away, pausing at other tables, exchanging a word here and there, friendly, good-humoured, the perfect hostess. Only when the depressed waiter clumsily dropped a dish did her aspect suddenly change to one of anger. She spoke only one word to him but he seemed to cringe. The señora, it was obvious, was something of a spitfire on occasion.

Later that evening Cade was sitting in the lounge when the yellow-haired man approached and introduced himself.

"My name's Johnson. Earl Johnson. I'm from the States. Philadelphia. Mind if I sit here?"

"Not at all. I'm Robert Cade."

"English, huh?"

"Yes."

"Thought you were. Saw you at dinner. Said to myself: There's a Limey or my name's not Earl Johnson. No offence meant. You got the look."

"Mrs. Torres thought I was American."

"That so? I'd have said she was sharper than that."

" I think she's pretty sharp just the same. Sharp enough to bring me to her hotel."

"Oh, she's a good business woman. Knows how to run this place, and in a town like San Borja it can't be too easy to make it pay."

" It is hers then, not her husband's?"

Johnson laughed. " Jorge? He's just the boy around here. He belongs to the señora like everything else. He even has to ask her for money when he needs it. And he always needs it. Yes, sir."

So that was the situation. It explained why Torres had been so ready to take a bribe to keep his mouth shut about his conversation with Cade. No doubt he was very glad to augment his allowance. But it could cut both ways; it might be equally easy to bribe him to open his mouth.

" You've been here some time then?" Cade asked.

" Couple of weeks." He summoned the waiter. " What are you drinking, Mr. Cade? They've got some good Scotch."

" Thanks," Cade said. " I'll have a Scotch and soda."

Johnson gave the order. " I'm a geologist," he said. " Working for an oil company."

" You think there may be oil in this area?"

" That's the sixty-four thousand dollar question. I'm here to get the answer. It's always a guess, mind you; never can tell for certain until they put those drills down and the black stuff comes spouting up."

The drinks came. Cade wondered whether Señora Torres ordered her Scotch in Caracas and had it flown in by the Dakota. It seemed probable. No doubt she had been returning from a foraging expedition when he had met her.

"What's your line of business?" Johnson asked. "That's if it's not a trade secret."

"No secret," Cade said. "I'm a journalist."

Johnson looked startled. "Oh, oh, I've been shooting my big mouth off too much. I hope you won't mention my work in anything you write. Don't want publicity just yet. You know how it is in the oil world; it only wants the rumour to get around and whoopee."

"Don't worry," Cade said. "I'm not a newshound. I'm doing a kind of geographical feature for a magazine. To tell you the truth, it may never see the light of day."

Johnson seemed relieved. "You sure had me worried there for a minute." He tapped his chin with his knuckles. "Look, Rob—okay if I call you that?"

"Okay," Cade said.

"I could maybe give you some help, Rob. I've got a jeep. I get around. You want to tag along any time, just say the word."

"Thanks," Cade said. "I might take you up on that. Do you know where the Gomara estate is?"

Johnson's eyes narrowed a shade. "Sure I know where it is. Going right past it tomorrow morning. You got some interest in Gomara?"

"Not particularly."

"If you're thinking of getting a story out of him, forget it. He sees nobody. And I mean nobody."

"No harm in trying."

"Well, if you like being warned off—"

Cade wondered whether Johnson himself had been warned off. Perhaps he had tried to do some prospecting

on the Gomara place and Gomara had objected. If he
really was as retiring as Torres had said, the last thing
he would want would be oilmen running all over his
estate.

" I'll risk it," he said.

" So be it then. I'll take you out there in the morning."

" Will Mrs. Johnson be going with you?" Cade
asked.

Johnson stared. " Come again."

" Your wife. Will she be going too?"

" I'm not married," Johnson said.

Cade saw that he had jumped to the wrong conclusion. " Oh, I thought—"

Johnson laughed. " You thought the lovely lady I was
dining with was my wife?"

" Yes."

" Not so. That was Miss Juanita Suarez."

" American?"

" South American. And speaking of angels, there she
is."

She had just come through the archway connecting
the lounge with the lobby. She was not really tall and
yet she gave the impression of being so; perhaps it was
in the way she carried herself; she moved across to
where they were sitting. Both men rose to their feet.

" Let me introduce Robert Cade," Johnson said.
" From England."

Miss Suarez smiled. At close quarters her beauty took
Cade's breath away. " I am so pleased to meet you, Mr.
Cade." She regarded him steadily with her dark, brilliant
eyes. " You have an interesting face. The bone structure

particularly. And very male. Oh, yes, extremely male. Don't you agree, Earl?"

"Sure," Johnson said. "He'd never make a female impersonator. That's one profession ruled out."

Cade felt slightly embarrassed. Miss Suarez was nothing if not direct.

Johnson noticed his embarrassment and gave a laugh. "Juanita is an artist. She looks at people with the eye of a painter. To her everybody is a potential model."

"Some day," Miss Suarez said, "I should like to paint you, Mr. Cade."

Looking at Miss Suarez Cade also felt that it might not be such a bad idea.

FIVE

THE GOMARA PLACE

THE JEEP was on the forecourt in front of the hotel when Cade went out. Johnson was standing beside it talking to Juanita Suarez. Miss Suarez was wearing blue jeans and a loose cotton shirt. She was able to look glamorous even in those clothes.

" Juanita is coming along too," Johnson said. " She's going to do some location painting."

Cade saw that Miss Suarez was carrying a folded easel, a paint-box and other gear. She began to pile all this into the back of the jeep.

" Leave room for the passenger," Johnson said. " You don't mind riding in the back, Rob?"

" Suits me fine," Cade said.

The day was warming up. There were no old men lying under the tree in the Plaza; no children there either. Perhaps the old men were still in bed, the children at school. Pancho brought a basket of provisions out of the hotel and handed it to Johnson.

" Okay then," Johnson said, " Let's go."

They got in. Johnson started the engine. They were

away. Nothing much seemed to be happening in the town; it was difficult to see for what reason it had grown there. Cade remarked on this to Johnson and the American explained.

" Used to be a silver mine in the foothills. It petered out years ago. There's still a bit of cattle raising, but if you ask me this is a dying town. Only thing that could put new life into it would be some industry."

" Like oil?"

" Like oil," Johnson said.

" And that would spoil it," Juanita said.

" Better spoilt than dead."

It did not take them long to get clear of the town. On the outskirts were huddles of adobe houses and wooden hovels, lines of washing hung out to dry in the hot sun. The jeep went past, leaving a cloud of dust in its wake. Then they were in open country, the road nothing but a stony trail, on each side the land covered with coarse tufts of grass with here and there clumps of trees and a few long-horned cattle grazing. In the distance ahead were the foothills and then the mountains.

They had been travelling for about half an hour when Johnson brought the jeep to a halt.

" There's the Gomara place."

There was a side-road branching off to the right. It was dead straight and it went gently downhill for about a quarter of a mile. The Gomara place was at the end of it : a big square house, two-storied, a few outbuildings and a clump of trees at the back, the whole enclosed by a fence, geometrically rectangular in outline. There was not another house anywhere in sight.

" Not troubled with the neighbours," Johnson remarked drily.

Juanita looked at the distant buildings, at the bleak
surrounding country, gave a little shudder. " It is so
desolate. So very desolate."

She had the right expression, Cade thought. There
was indeed a sense of desolation. The poor, coarse grass
with areas of dry, stony soil showing through, the occa-
sional gnarled, ragged-looking tree, the vast distances, all
combined to give an impression of a land untamed and
untameable, a wilderness, inimical to human life.

" Why should a man choose to come and live here?"
Cade asked.

Johnson gave him a swift, sidelong glance. " It makes
a good refuge."

" From what?"

" The world."

" You think Gomara is running from something?"

" He is not running," Juanita said. " He has stopped."

Cade looked at Johnson. " But you think that this is
his bolthole?"

" I don't know Gomara. Anyway, he didn't build the
place. From all accounts he's only been here a few years.
It was originally a cattle ranch, an estancia, but it's not
really good cattle country. About the only breed that
can stand the conditions is the Spanish Longhorn, and
you can't run more than one cow to every fifty acres.
That's a lot of land per cow."

Johnson seemed to have been studying the subject. It
hardly appeared to have much to do with oil.

" But Gomara doesn't raise cattle," Cade said.

" Who told you that?"

" Jorge Torres said he had retired."

" Very much so. Well, I'll take you to the gate, but I don't think you'll get in."

" Don't bother. I'll walk the rest of the way," Cade said. He got out of the jeep.

" If they don't let you in you'll have a long walk back. I'm going to the hills."

" I'll risk it."

" I'll be back this way around four."

" Right," Cade said. " If I'm not here, don't worry. I'll have made my own way into town."

" Well, if that's the way you want it."

As he set off down the road he heard the jeep move away. The sun was hot and he began to sweat. In the distance beyond the house he caught sight of a rider on a black horse; there was no other sign of life. When he drew nearer he could see that the fence was of heavy chain-link wire-netting to a height of eight feet or so, topped with several strands of barbed wire. There was a tall iron gate at the entrance with vertical bars ending in sharp spikes at the top. It was quite evident that Gomara believed in being in a position to deny admittance to any unwanted visitor.

The gate was closed. On the other side the road went past a large timber building that could have been a barn or stable. The house stood further back, perhaps fifty yards from the entrance. There was a chain on the gate fastened with a padlock. Cade looked for someone to let him in and could see no one. He rattled the chain. No one came to see who was making the noise. The Gomara place seemed as desolate as the surrounding country.

Cade searched for some means of announcing his

presence. There ought to have been a bell, but there was nothing of the kind. He decided to shout. After he had been shouting and rattling the gate for about half a minute a man appeared from the building on the right. He had a dark, tanned face and a sullen expression. He looked like a vaquero. He came to the gate and stared at Cade through the bars.

" What do you want?" His voice was harsh and unwelcoming.

" I want to come in," Cade said.

" Why?"

" I wish to see Señor Gomara."

" Señor Gomara sees no one. Go away."

" I have come a long way to see him."

" That is your concern. I did not ask you to come."

" Will you take a message to Señor Gomara?"

" It would be useless. A waste of time."

The man was wearing a sweat-stained sombrero, a check shirt, baggy trousers thrust into short riding-boots and a leather belt adorned with brass studs. His hair was greying slightly at the sides and he looked as tough as a rawhide whip.

" You could at least tell Señor Gomara that I am here."

" He would not be interested."

" How do you know?"

" I have my orders."

It was his final word. He was turning away when Cade heard the sound of horse's hoofs.

A woman's voice said: " Unlock the gate for me, José."

Cade swung round. It was the rider he had seen in

the distance, the rider on the black horse. She was wearing a black Spanish hat with a wide flat brim and silver nuggets in the band. She had jodhpurs and a white silk shirt. She had long legs and a slim waist, and her breasts were firm and pointed.

José came back to the gate, took a key from his pocket and unlocked the padlock. The girl pushed the hat back from her head and let it hang by the chin-cord. She had short blonde hair and at first glance she seemed almost childishly young; not quite so young on a closer examination. But at first or second or any other glance she was worth looking at; of that there could be no doubt whatever. Cade looked at her and could see only one point to criticise : there was a suggestion of petulance about the mouth; it was the mouth of a spoilt child.

" Who are you?" she demanded.

" Robert Cade."

She stared at him coolly while José swung open the gate. " And what are you doing here, Robert Cade?" She was speaking Spanish but it did not sound like her native language. She could well have come from the same part of the world as Earl Johnson.

" I want to see Señor Gomara."

" But Señor Gomara does not want to see you."

" I told him," José said. " I told him the master would see no one."

" So now you must go away, Robert Cade," the girl said. " You have had a long walk for nothing in this hot sun." There was a note of mockery in her voice and mockery in her eyes also. The eyes were large, blue, of an innocence that was perhaps misleading. " You should have brought a horse. Or perhaps you do not ride."

"I ride when there is something to ride," Cade said. "I have ridden with gauchos."

"Gauchos!" she said, and the mockery was gone from her voice. The word seemed to have touched some nerve. She looked at him more keenly. "Where have you ridden with gauchos?"

"On the pampas of Argentina. On the estancia of a man named Oviedo. I and a friend."

"Who are you?" she asked a second time.

"I told you. I am Robert Cade." But he knew that she was asking more than that.

The black horse lifted its head and jingled the curb chains. José stood with his hand on the gate and looked impatient.

"What do you want with Gomara?"

"I have a message," Cade said.

"A message? From whom?"

Cade lowered his voice so that José should not hear. "From Harry Banner."

He had been feeling his way, playing it blind. But he was hitting the right notes. The girl's eyes seemed to light up. She got down from the horse and handed the reins to José.

"Take him to the stable. Señor Cade will come with me."

"My orders are to let no one in," José said stubbornly.

She answered with a flash of anger: "Your orders are not to argue with me."

José stood his ground. "I do as the master says."

"You do also as I say."

"I do not take orders from a woman."

"Let me pass."

" Not with this man."

She was carrying a riding-switch in her hand. She raised it and struck him on the left cheek. " Stand out of my way. You are being insolent."

For a moment it seemed to Cade that José was going to retaliate. His eyes glittered angrily and he took half a pace forward. Then he controlled himself. " As you wish, señorita." He moved to one side, taking the horse with him.

She walked past José and Cade followed. As he passed José he glanced at the man's face. José was slowly rubbing his cheek where the switch had lashed it and there was hatred in his smouldering eyes. One thing was certain if nothing else : this was no friend.

The house was built of wood and painted white. There was a portico and a few steps leading up to the front door. The door was big and heavy with black iron hinges and a twisted wrought-iron ring instead of a doorknob. The girl climbed the steps, pushed open the door and went in through the wide doorway, Cade still following.

It was a spacious entrance hall. Whoever had built the house had done things on a grand scale; perhaps when the silver mine had been in production the estancia had been prosperous also. There was a broad staircase leading up out of the hall, tall, curtained windows, opulent furnishing. It appeared that Gomara did not lack money either.

The girl conducted Cade to a drawing-room and invited him to sit down. There were armchairs and sofas upholstered in rich brocade, polished tables, oil paintings in gilded frames. Cade sat in one of the chairs.

"We may as well speak English," the girl said. "I'm American." She laid her switch on one of the tables, took off the Spanish hat and laid that on the table also.

"Yes," Cade said.

"You knew that of course."

Cade said nothing.

"You are a friend of Harry's?"

"Yes."

She sat on the arm of a chair, facing Cade and swinging one jodhpur-clad leg. "I am Della Lindsay."

"Yes," Cade said again.

"You knew that too of course. He'll have told you about me."

Cade looked at her.

"The message is for me, isn't it. Not for Carlos."

"Were you expecting a message, Miss Lindsay?"

"Oh, look," she said, "you don't have to play it so cool. I told you who I am. What do you want—my fingerprints?"

"I don't think that will be necessary."

"Everything's okay, isn't it? He didn't run into any trouble?"

"No trouble," Cade said.

"Where is he?"

"In London."

"That's fine. That really is great. I always wanted to go to England. I've been around but never there."

"It's a nice country," Cade said. He was still feeling his way. Della Lindsay was a surprise, something he had not bargained for. And yet he might have guessed there would be a woman involved, knowing Harry Banner. The question was, just how did she fit in?

It was warm and close in the room. It had the feel of a room that was not much used. Cade wondered where Gomara was.

" When does he want me to join him in London?" the girl asked.

" Not yet," Cade said. " It's not all straightened out yet. Give it time."

She looked disappointed; the corners of her mouth drooped. " I don't see what there is to straighten out. You said there'd been no trouble. My God, I wish he'd hurry. I'm sick of this place. Might as well be buried alive."

" Why did you come here?"

She shot him a glance. " Are you kidding? What would a girl like me go anywhere with a guy like Carlos for if it wasn't the money? He has to have a woman around. I guess he always did. Maybe it'd have been better for him if he hadn't."

" I'd like to talk to him," Cade said.

" I don't see what you want to talk to him about."

" Call it a whim."

" Funny kind of a whim." She sounded faintly suspicious. " Anyway, he won't see you. He's not pleased, you know."

" No?"

" Well, it's not surprising, is it? You could hardly expect him to be shouting for joy. Besides, I think he's afraid Harry may not stick to his side of the bargain."

" He's got nothing to fear from Harry."

" That's what I tell him, but he doesn't believe it. He doesn't trust anyone."

" Not even you?"

She laughed. "Carlos is not a fool. Know what he once told me? Loyalty is measured in dollars. He could be right at that."

"It's cynical philosophy," Cade said. "Are you sure you couldn't persuade him to see me?"

"You're really set on it, aren't you?"

"Yes."

"Well," she said doubtfully, "I can try. But it won't be any use today; he'll have to be worked round to the idea gradually. Can you come back tomorrow?"

"I'll do that."

"Am I to tell him you know Harry?"

Cade thought that one over before answering. Then he said : "No, better not."

"I think you're right," Della said. "Tell him that and he'd fly through the roof." She gave him a long, cool stare, faintly puzzled, it seemed. "I don't altogether get you, Mr. Cade. What's in this for you? What are you getting out of it?"

"Just call it a kick," Cade said. "Yes, just call it that."

"Where are you staying?"

"At the Phoenix in San Borja."

"Harry stayed there for a while."

"Yes, I know," Cade said. He wondered whether she knew about the other two men, about Manuel Lopez and Luis Guzman. "Then he came to work here. Is that right?"

"I imagine he told you."

"He didn't tell me how he got the job."

She smiled. "Harry's a very persuasive man. He talked Carlos into it."

He had talked her into something too, and Cade would have liked to know just what. But perhaps it had not needed much talking in her case.

" What exactly did he do?"

" Didn't he tell you?"

" He told me he was a kind of man about the place. Maybe a handyman."

She gave a laugh. " That could describe it. Handy with a gun maybe. He was Carlos's bodyguard."

" I see." And yet he did not see, not with complete clarity. He would have liked to ask more questions but decided that it might not be advisable to do so. Better not to let the girl know just how much in the dark he was. Perhaps there would be a bit more light when he had seen Gomara. If he saw Gomara.

" How did you get out here?" Della asked. " You didn't walk from San Borja, did you?"

" Not all the way. A man named Earl Johnson gave me a lift in his jeep." He was about to add that Johnson was prospecting for oil, then remembered that Johnson had asked him to keep that business under his hat. He need not have worried.

" Oh, that oil man," Della said. " He's been around here. Wanted to do some soundings or something on the place. Carlos sent him packing."

" He saw Gomara?"

" No. He didn't get past the gate. But he got the message. Is he going to take you back to San Borja?"

" If I'm at the road junction at four o'clock."

" You expected to be here as long as that?"

" I didn't expect anything. I took a chance."

She looked thoughtful for a moment; then she said :

" You could stay until afternoon but I think it would be better if you didn't. If you like I'll take you back to town in the car."

" That's very good of you."

" Don't let it go to your head," Della said. " There's some things I have to do in town."

SIX

TORRES ASKS FOR MORE

CADE WAS in the Phoenix lounge when Earl Johnson walked in. There was no sign of Juanita Suarez and Cade supposed that she had gone to her room. Johnson looked hot and dusty.

"Glad to see you got back okay, Rob. I was a shade worried when you weren't at the rendezvous. Did you walk?"

"No, I was brought back in style. In a Mercedes."

"You don't say. Whose?"

"Gomara's."

Johnson looked incredulous. "You saw him?"

"No. I saw Miss Lindsay instead. She drove the Mercedes. And a pretty good driver too."

"Miss Lindsay! You mean that blonde he keeps around the place for decoration?"

"None other."

Johnson tapped himself on the chin. He spoke with a certain grudging admiration. "Well, I have to hand it to you, Rob; you're a fast worker. I didn't even make first base."

"So she told me. Maybe you didn't use the right technique."

"Maybe I didn't. Like to teach me yours?"

"Some day," Cade said. "Not now."

"I may hold you to that promise. The blonde is really quite a dish."

"So you've seen Miss Lindsay?"

"In town. I've never spoken to her."

"Did she come with Gomara when he took the place?"

"So I heard. The story is she was on the stage. A stripper maybe. I don't think anybody really knows. They just make up these tales."

"It could be true just the same; she's got the attributes. Where did they come from?"

"Who knows? Gomara is a mystery man. Nobody even gets to see him."

"I may get to see him tomorrow."

Johnson whistled softly. "How'd you manage that?"

"I did a little work on Della Lindsay and she's going to do a little work on Gomara—on my behalf."

This time there was a trace of envy mixed with Johnson's admiration. "Well, I'll be hung. You sure do know your way around, Mr. Cade. I'd have laid a hundred to one in dollars you wouldn't get past the gate, but oh, how wrong I was. Let me buy you a drink."

"No," Cade said. "Let me buy you one. You look as though you need it."

At dinner Miss Suarez looked cool and poised, as though utterly unaffected by the dust and heat of her expedition to the hills. Cade willingly accepted an invitation to join her and Johnson at their table.

" Might as well be sociable," Johnson said. " We Anglo-Saxons ought to stick together."

" I am not an Anglo-Saxon," Miss Suarez said.

It was an unnecessary protestation, Cade thought. Anyone less like an Anglo-Saxon would have been difficult to imagine.

" We'll elect you an honorary member of the club," Johnson said. " No entrance fee."

She gave a small mock bow, smiling. " I am deeply grateful for the honour."

" Have you had a successful day, Miss Suarez?" Cade asked.

She made a gesture with the fingers of her right hand, as graceful as the flutter of a butterfly's wings. " Oh, call me Juanita. We are friends, I hope. Yes, I have had a good day. In the mountains the only problem is in deciding which of so many excellent subjects to choose. One regrets too that one is not more talented with the brush."

" Now you are being too modest," Johnson said. " Incidentally, our friend Rob has also had a successful expedition."

She glanced quickly at Cade and he was surprised at the keen interest she showed. " You saw Señor Gomara? You actually saw the hermit?"

" No," Cade said. " I was not quite so successful as that. But I went into the house."

" He has ingratiated himself with Gomara's blonde," Johnson said. " She's going to arrange an interview with the man himself."

" She's going to try. She didn't promise anything. Gomara may be difficult."

Johnson grinned. " Judging by her looks, that baby could persuade the President of the United States to vote communist."

Miss Suarez regarded Cade with her softly glowing eyes. " You have perhaps fallen a little for this Miss Lindsay? Is it not so, Roberto?" She was gently teasing, but behind the teasing Cade seemed to detect a more serious note. Both she and Johnson had a keener interest in Gomara than could have been explained by mere idle curiosity. He wondered why this should be.

But when he answered it was in the same light bantering tone that Miss Suarez had used. " Not so, Juanita. Gentlemen may prefer blondes, but I am no gentleman. My taste is rather for the darker type."

She smiled. " No gentleman perhaps, but most certainly a diplomat."

Earl Johnson looked amused.

Cade went to his room after dinner. He was staring down into the Plaza when he heard a gentle tap on the door.

" Come in," he said, turning away from the window.

The door opened immediately and Jorge Torres slipped into the room. He closed the door and stood with his back to it, looking at Cade, saying nothing.

" What is it?" Cade asked. " What do you want?"

Torres smiled ingratiatingly, but there was a certain cunning calculation in his smile and also in the shifty eyes. It was as though he were weighing Cade up.

" I wish to talk with you, señor."

" On what subject?"

Torres moved away from the door and rubbed his

hands together as though washing them with invisible soap and water. " On the subject of money perhaps."

" Always an interesting subject," Cade said, and waited for Torres to be more specific.

Torres stopped washing his hands and fiddled with the ends of his moustache; his gaze wandered about the room, fell on Cade in passing and flickered away again. " Yesterday, señor, we had an interesting conversation. You asked me questions about certain people—Señor Banner, Señor Gomara, two other men. You did not wish me to speak of this conversation; you gave me a small token to remind me not to speak of it."

" So? " Cade said.

" Today another person also asks me questions."

" About what?"

" About you, señor."

" Is that so?"

" Yes, señor. But of course I say that I know nothing. I forget all about those things you ask me. I remember the small token and I remember to forget."

" Good," Cade said.

Torres's gaze fell upon Cade and this time it did not move away. " Not so good perhaps. I could have earned a little money if I had talked, if I had not remembered to forget. Another time it might be more difficult unless I have another token to remind me."

Cade saw how it was : Torres had spotted a possibility of making some more easy money. The story he had just spun might well be true; possibly Johnson or Miss Suarez had asked questions. But what if they had? It made little difference whether or not they knew of his interest in Harry Banner. As far as he was concerned all that really mattered was to find out how Banner had come by the diamonds that were now in Holden Bales's keeping and why he had been killed. It had been a mistake in the first place to bribe Torres to keep his mouth shut about the conversation; it had merely roused the man's curiosity; but he was certainly not going to let Torres extract any more bolivars from his pocket. The señora had warned him not to give money to her husband and in future he would heed that warning.

" You'll get no more tokens from me," he said.

Torres looked disappointed. " That is unfortunate, señor. Without the token my memory cannot be relied upon; indeed, it will be most unreliable. I may forget not to mention what we have spoken about."

" Señor Torres," Cade said, " you may go to the devil."

Torres shrugged. " Eventually perhaps, but not immediately. And I think you would be well advised to help my memory with another token, because it is not only our conversation that I might forget not to talk about. There is now another matter of some importance."

Cade glanced at him. There was an unmistakable threat in Torres's voice. " What other matter?"

" Shall we say, for example, the small gun that you have in your bag?"

So that was it. Torres had been snooping through his luggage while he had been away from the hotel and had found the gun. Well, it was only what might have been expected of such a man. The gun was a .38 revolver with a stubby barrel; he had bought it in Caracas on a sudden impulse. He did not imagine he would need a gun, but it was not beyond the bounds of possibility that he might. Harry Banner could have used a gun in London; it might have saved him from being killed. And the people who had killed Banner were still at large, unless Superintendent Alletson had made an arrest in the last day or two; and he did not think that likely. All things considered, a gun might not be altogether superfluous; a gun and one box of .38 ammunition.

"You have been searching my luggage."

"The bag was not locked."

"Does that give you the right to stick your nose in it?"

"The right? Perhaps not. The opportunity—certainly. Do you wish me to keep silent about the small gun, señor?"

"I am telling you to do so," Cade said.

There was a greedy look in Torres's eye. "Without some incentive that might well be impossible. How do I know that you have not come here to kill Señor Gomara for example? Perhaps I should warn him."

"Perhaps you should mind your own business," Cade said. He was becoming a little tired of Jorge Torres. On one point his mind was now made up : gun or no gun, Torres would get no more bribes out of him. That talk of going to Gomara was probably nothing but an idle threat anyway. And even if he did go, why should Gomara believe such a fantastic story? Unless, of course, it was the kind of thing that Gomara was expecting, the reason why he had hidden himself away and felt the need for a bodyguard.

"But," Torres said, "this is my business. Be sensible, señor. Give me another fifty bolivars and I guarantee that my tongue will be as still as a sleeping lizard."

Cade advanced two paces very sharply, seized Torres's right arm and twisted it savagely up behind his back. Torres gave a cry of pain.

"If you are wise," Cade said, speaking directly into Torres's ear, "you will keep a still tongue in your head anyway. I am a patient man but my patience is not inexhaustible. Do you understand?"

Torres tried to get free, cursing. Cade twisted the arm a little more, making Torres cry out again.

"Do you understand?"

"I understand," Torres gasped. "I will say nothing. Depend upon it. Only let me go. I will not say a word. I promise."

"You had better not."

Cade gave Torres a push and released the arm. Torres fell face downward on the bed and got up slowly, looking as venomous as a cobra. He had been hurt and he had been humiliated, and if the opportunity ever came his way to do Cade an injury there was little doubt that he would seize it. Cade knew this; he knew that he had perhaps acted rather too hastily and had made an enemy. Twisting Torres's arm would not even make the man hold his tongue; it had served no useful purpose at all except to relieve Cade's anger. It would perhaps have been better to fork out the fifty bolivars.

Torres retreated to the door and there was hatred in his eyes. He massaged his right arm. "Señor Cade," he said, "you should not have done that."

"You asked for it."

"I did not ask for it and you should not have done it."

" Go away," Cade said.

Torres opened the door. " I will go now, but later there may be a reckoning, and then you may be sorry for what you have just done to me."

He went out of the room and closed the door very softly behind him.

Cade saw no more of Jorge Torres that evening, but he saw Maria Torres. He wanted her advice.

" I wish to hire a car. Do you know where I can get one in San Borja?"

" A car with a driver or one to drive yourself?"

" To drive myself."

Señora Torres considered the matter for a moment, then said : " You had better go and see Martin Duero. He may be able to provide you with what you need."

" Where do I find this Señor Duero?"

Señora Torres went into detailed directions. They sounded complicated. " Do you think you can find your way now?"

" I doubt it."

" Perhaps it would be better if I found a boy to take you there."

" I think it would be much better," Cade said. " Can you do that?"

" But of course, señor."

" Tell him to be here after breakfast tomorrow."

The boy had been burnt so deeply by the sun that he was almost black. His name was Pablo and he was ten years old. When he grew up, so he informed Cade in all seriousness, he was going to emigrate to the United

States and become an astronaut. He was fascinated by the stars and space travel.

"You think they will take me, señor?"

"Why not, Pablo? They're always looking for good men. Maybe you'll be the first man to land on Venus."

The boy's eyes shone like precious stones. "I cannot wait to grow up. Why don't the years go faster?"

"One day you'll wish they didn't go so fast," Cade said.

They crossed the Plaza, walked through a narrow alleyway where some plump, black-haired women were gossiping, and came out on to what could have been the main street of the town. There were some shops, some motor lorries, a few cars, people.

"This way, señor," Pablo said.

They turned to the left, continued on for about two hundred yards, then plunged down another alleyway and came suddenly on a patch of waste ground where an old Chrysler convertible had come to the end of its journeys. It stood there rusting gently, with no tyres and the hood nothing but a skeleton. Some small fry were sitting in it and they were not even squabbling; perhaps in imagination they were driving down the shining streets of Caracas with all the glittering shops and nightclubs and hotels on either side.

"They're going places," Cade said.

Pablo looked infinitely contemptuous. "Children's games," he said with all the superiority of one who was ten years old and going to be an astronaut.

It turned out to be a rough timber building with no paint and a corrugated iron roof. It had the smell of oil and rubber that you get wherever motor vehicles congregate. There were half a dozen cars of various ages and conditions, none very new, and there were two Italian scooters with worn saddles and smooth tyres. A man was working at a bench on the left as you went in; he was filing a piece of metal held in a vice and drops of sweat were falling on to it from his forehead. He was not much more than five feet tall and as fat as a leg of pork. He was standing on a box to give him added height.

"That is Señor Duero," Pablo said.

"Thanks, Pablo. You've been a lot of help." Cade felt in his pocket, pulled out some coins and gave them to the boy. "I can manage now. See you on Venus."

"On Venus," the boy said. He stowed the coins in his pocket and went away whistling.

Duero stopped filing and looked at Cade. He did not get off the box; perhaps it gave him confidence.

"You want something, señor?"

"A car," Cade said.

Duero said, a note of surprise and hope in his voice : "You wish to buy a car?"

"Not to buy. I want to hire one."

Duero looked both disappointed and doubtful. "You wish to drive this car yourself?"

"Yes."

"I do not know you, señor. To let a stranger have a car, it is a risk."

"I am a good driver."

"I do not doubt it."

"Señora Torres told me to come to you."

Duero's expression changed immediately. Suddenly he seemed to be a great deal happier. "You are staying at the Phoenix?"

"Yes. My name is Cade."

"Ah, that is different." Duero got off the box and waddled towards Cade. He wiped his right hand on the seat of his trousers and held it out to Cade. Cade shook it. It felt like a thick slice of raw bacon that had been left out in the sun. "Anyone that is recommended by Señora Torres, him I trust. Do you wish to go far?"

"No, not far."

Duero looked as though he would have liked to ask Cade where he was going, but he suppressed the desire. He waddled across to a Citroen saloon, the kind that the Citroen people had turned out in tens of thousands to populate the roads of France, not the new model but the old one that looked like a car.

Duero kicked the tyres, each one in turn, as though to demonstrate that he was above favouritism. He put both hands on the side of the body and rocked it on its springs, producing a harsh, grating noise.

"Good car."

"How much?" Cade asked.

Duero got into the driving seat, started the engine. He revved up and thick smoke poured from the exhaust. He switched off and got out. He patted the bonnet with his hand as if it had been a god.

"Good engine too."

"How much?"

Duero pursed his lips and looked like a man who is reluctant to bring sordid financial considerations into a pleasant conversation but is forced to do so.

"Fifty bolivars a day—and the petrol."

"Fill the tank," Cade said.

SEVEN

THE SNAKE PIT

IT WAS not, Cade had to admit, as good a car as the Mercedes he had travelled in the previous day. The upholstery had suffered from the ravages of time and hard use, and there were a lot of noises that had certainly not been there when the car had been younger. These noises became louder when they had left the town and were out on the road that led to the Gomara place. Fortunately, the engine, despite the exhaust smoke, seemed to be in fair condition, and though the steering had a nasty habit of pulling over to the left, Cade soon got used to this and fought it with appropriate pressure on the wheel.

It was about mid-morning when he came to the road junction. He made the right turn and drove at a moderate speed towards the gate in the fence that ringed the house and outbuildings. José must have seen him coming for he had already released the padlock when Cade pulled up. He swung the gate open and walked to the car, peering in at Cade as though to make certain it was in fact he. After a momentary examination he appeared to be satisfied if not pleased.

" I have orders to let you in, señor."

" Thank you," Cade said.

" You do not have to thank me." José's tone and his expression seemed to indicate that he regarded any thanks as an insult. " It is not my decision. For myself I would have left the gate locked; but I have to obey orders."

Cade wondered why the man should be so ill-tempered. Perhaps he was still smarting from the lash of Della Lindsay's riding-switch and associated Cade with that humiliation. Or perhaps he was just naturally ill-disposed to the rest of mankind. Anyway, Cade was not bothered about José; he was more interested in meeting Gomara.

He let in the clutch and drove slowly through the gateway, past the big stable building and up to the front of the house. The girl had also seen him coming, and it was she who opened the door to him.

She said : " I see you got yourself a car."

" It was either that or a horse."

She closed the door behind him. " I had a hard time persuading Carlos to see you. You wouldn't believe. You aren't carrying a gun, are you?"

" A gun?"

" He told me to make sure. He doesn't like men who carry guns."

" Who does?" Cade said. " But don't worry. I'm clean. You can frisk me if you like." He had left the Colt in his bag at the hotel. He had thought of bringing it and had decided not to. Perhaps it was as well in the circumstances.

The girl gave him a long, cool stare. She had just the right amount of sun-tan for a blonde and she was not the kind who came out in freckles. With that face and that figure she certainly had all the makings of a stripper; it was easy to see how the rumours had got started in San Borja.

" Maybe you'd enjoy that," she said.

" Maybe I would," Cade said.

But she did not give him the pleasure. " I'll take your word, Mr. Cade. Come along. It's this way."

They went down a corridor, carpeted, their feet falling silently as if on turf. From somewhere came a smell of cooking, but there was a stillness about the house, an impression of life having stopped; it was like a retreat where you waited to die. Della Lindsay did not really fit in; you could not imagine her waiting to die.

They came to a door and she paused with her hand resting on the knob, " Be careful what you say to him."

" I'll be careful," Cade promised.

She opened the door. " Go in then."

Cade walked in. He had expected Della to follow, but instead he heard the sound of the door closing and when he turned he saw that she had gone away and left him to it.

It was an unusual kind of room to say the least. It was much longer than it was wide and at the far end it opened off to the right, apparently L-shaped. It was stiflingly hot and close and completely devoid of any furnishing. There were no windows, but a subdued greenish illumination came in through skylights in the lofty roof, rather like the light in deep jungle. The floor was of concrete, quite bare, and down the centre ran a wide, shallow pit. The sides of the pit were concave with an overhanging lip, like a cliff undermined by the sea. In the pit were rocks and boulders, pools of stagnant water, logs of wood and a number of plants and bushes growing in patches of soil.

There were other things in the pit too; Cade saw them when he went to the edge and looked down. Some were gliding sinuously on mysterious errands known only to themselves, others were motionless, coiled and sleeping, their skins gleaming like metal. Snakes.

He could understand then why Della had not come in with him. She was probably not a lover of snakes. He was not sure that he was himself.

He was still looking down into the pit when he heard a sound like the whine of an electric motor. He turned and saw a man approaching in a wheeled chair which must have come from the other part of the room beyond the angle. It stopped about six feet from Cade and the man stared at him. He was wearing a loose linen suit, and he was very thin and his hair was white. His face looked fallen-in all over; even his temples had a hollowed-out appearance; it was as though there were a vacuum inside that was sucking down all the surface areas and revealing the bony structure like the peaks and ridges of a mountain range. His hands also were thin and bony, and the veins stood out like blue cords. In the left hand he was holding a small automatic pistol. It looked to Cade like a .25 calibre. It was pointed at him.

"Señor Cade, I believe," the man said. His voice too was thin, like a whisper; it seemed as drained, as bloodless as the man himself.

"Yes," Cade said. "You don't need the gun, Señor Gomara."

"I am a cautious man," Gomara said. "But no doubt you have already heard that. There may not be many more years of life remaining to me but I should not wish to have them shortened."

"Is that probable?"

"Probable? Who knows?" He lowered the pistol and let it lie in his lap. "Della tells me that you have a great desire to see me."

"Yes," Cade said.

Gomara had changed. He had grown older; older by more than the mere extent of the years that had passed. He looked ill; perhaps was ill. When Cade had seen him last he had been black-haired, vigorous, full of life, enjoying it to the full. But that had been in Argentina, and his name had not been Gomara; it had been Rodriguez.

It had also been before the scandal.

Carlos Rodriguez had been an important member of the Argentine government at that time. In his capacity as a newspaperman Cade had seen a good deal of Rodriguez; Rodriguez had been much in the public eye. There had also been numerous press conferences which Cade had attended.

Carlos Rodriguez had been near the top and still rising when the bubble burst. And when the revelation came it was not merely the revelation of a corrupt politician's shady financial dealings, of the bribery concerning government contracts, though this was bad enough. No; there was also the scandal of his private life. There were reports of wild orgies on Rodriguez's country estate, of sexual perversions, of the seduction of young girls, of drug-taking. And then there was the matter of Isabella Martinez, whose naked body had been found floating in Rodriguez's swimming-pool.

It had, of course, been the end of his political career, but he had had powerful friends and much money. Before the police could take him he had disappeared, no one knew where. The Rodriguez Affair, as it was called, made news for weeks as more and more unsavoury details came to light, but the chief actor had already left the stage and did not return for the curtain call.

Cade could see now why Gomara was such a retiring man. There were many people who would have given much to learn of his whereabouts : the Argentine police would most certainly have been interested, and poor Isabella Martinez, that beautiful and unfortunate young girl, had had relations who, if they ever found the man who had corrupted her and had been the cause of her death, would undoubtedly take a terrible revenge.

" For what reason did you wish to see me?" Gomara asked.

He was, Cade estimated, not yet sixty years old, but he looked nearer eighty. Perhaps he had contracted some disease that had first crippled him and now was slowly killing him. Perhaps this was the punishment for the kind of life he had led.

" I am a journalist," Cade said.

Gomara looked startled. " Della did not tell me that. She told me that you had some important information to give me."

" I told her that. I am afraid it was a piece of subterfuge in order to get an interview with you."

Gomara's sunken eyes regarded Cade stonily, as though probing for the truth, and the fingers of his left hand strayed towards the butt of the pistol; but he did not pick it up.

" Why should you want an interview with me?"

Cade wondered whether Gomara had recognised him also. It was possible but not likely. At press conferences in Buenos Aires he had been only one of many; there was no reason why his features should have impressed themselves on Gomara's memory. Nevertheless, the possibility was there.

" I am writing a magazine feature—about this part of the country—the cattle rearing—"

" I do not rear cattle."

" But this was once a cattle estancia."

" I know nothing of that. It was before I came here."

" So you have not been here long?"

" Señor Cade," Gomara said, " I believe you know very well how long I have been here."

" I have made one or two enquiries," Cade admitted. " But one does not believe all one hears."

" That is so. One does not."

The heat in the room was really oppressive; sweat began to trickle down Cade's face. Gomara regarded him with a sardonic expression; he himself appeared quite cool; he looked desiccated, every drop of moisture already drawn out of him.

" You seem warm," he said. " Why not remove your jacket? I have no objection."

Cade took off his jacket and draped it over his arm.

" Are you a lover of snakes, Señor Cade?"

Cade stared down into the pit. There was that about the creatures in there which reminded him of his host : Gomara himself had something reptilian in him, and his eyes were as hard and cold as the eyes of a snake.

"To be perfectly honest," Cade said, "they make me sick."

"Is that so?" Gomara sounded surprised. "Yet to me they are irresistibly fascinating." He pointed his finger. "There, you see that one? That is a whipsnake from India. You can see how it got its name."

"Venomous?"

"Oh, yes, very deadly. As also is that annulated snake which is one of our native breeds. And of course the viper there."

"Did you make this collection?" Cade asked.

"No; it was here when I came. The original owner is dead. I am told that he got drunk one day and fell into the snake pit. Most unfortunate."

"Yes."

"There is an old man who looks after the snakes; his name is Andres. Do you mind pressing that button over there?"

It was a bell-push in the wall. Cade put his thumb on the button, then released it. A few seconds later a man came in, not by the door by which Cade had entered but by another at the far end of the room.

He was a Negro and very tall—six and a half feet at least, though he stooped a little. His head was bald and shining, and he had a white beard and a wide flat nose. His arms were long, hanging loosely at his sides, and he was so thin Cade almost expected to hear his bones rattling as he walked. He was wearing a white shirt, white cotton trousers and rawhide boots. He stopped when he reached Gomara's chair and stood there, saying nothing.

"I have been telling Señor Cade that you are the one who looks after the snakes, Andres. Señor Cade says that snakes make him sick."

The Negro said nothing, but he looked at Cade for a moment, then down into the pit.

"They do not make you sick, do they, Andres?"

"No, señor," the Negro said. He had a high, thin voice like a very old recording.

"Show Señor Cade how easy it is to handle snakes when you know the way," Gomara said.

Without a word the Negro lowered himself over the edge of the concrete and stepped into the pit. With a movement surprisingly rapid in one so old he stooped and picked up a snake, gripping it just below the head. The snake was about three feet long and its body was covered with shining brown spots like splashes of paint. The Negro carried it to the edge of the pit and held it out towards Cade. Cade involuntarily stepped back from that sinister head with its dripping fangs, its darting tongue and its bright cold eyes.

Gomara laughed. "Do not be afraid. The snake is quite harmless while Andres holds it."

"Does he ever get bitten?"

Gomara looked at the Negro. "You heard the question, Andres. Do the snakes ever bite you?"

The Negro grinned; there were no teeth in his mouth. "Me, señor? Why would they do that?" He held the snake close to his lips and kissed it. He put the head in his mouth, then drew it out slowly. "They are my friends, my children." He put the snake down and it wriggled away.

"You may go now, Andres," Gomara said.

The Negro climbed out of the pit and left the room.

"A remarkable old man," Gomara said. "He has a way with snakes. I should not advise anyone else to step down into that pit."

"Perhaps no one else would want to do so."

"Do you intend to write about what you have seen here?"

"Do you wish me to?"

"I think you would be very ill-advised to do anything of the kind," Gomara said. "I do not think there is anything here that would be of interest to your readers."

"Perhaps you are right."

"I know I am right." There could have been a hint of a threat in Gomara's whispering voice and in the cold snake's eyes. "Leave it, Señor Cade. Leave it alone. And now forgive me if I do not see you to the door. You can, I think, find your own way out."

He touched the lever on the chair and the motor whined. The chair turned and rolled smoothly away down the room. Cade walked to the door and opened it. He was glad to get out of that hot, slightly fetid atmosphere, away from the silent menace of the snake pit.

EIGHT

A TALK WITH DELLA

HE HAD almost reached the front door when he heard the girl's voice.

"Mr. Cade."

He turned. Della Lindsay had changed her dress during his interview with Gomara; the one she was wearing now was of a colour to match her hair; it was very simple, very chic, very short; it had probably cost quite a deal of money; that kind of simplicity usually did. Cade guessed that she bought her clothes in Caracas; he doubted whether there was any shop in San Borja that would have suited her tastes.

"I'd like to have a talk with you," she said.

Cade walked back towards her. "I'm always ready to have a talk with someone who looks as attractive as you, Miss Lindsay."

She frowned slightly. "You don't have to pull out the compliments for me. I'm not looking for flattery."

"No flattery," Cade said.

"And you can drop the Miss Lindsay. The name's Della."

" And mine's Robert."

" Okay, Robert. Let's go in here."

It was the room she had taken him into the previous day. Cade dropped his jacket on a table and sat down in one of the brocaded armchairs.

Della said : " So now you've seen Carlos. Are you satisfied?"

" I'm satisfied," Cade said.

" What do you think of him?"

" I think he's a very frightened man."

She asked quickly : " Why do you say that?"

" Who but a frightened man would carry a gun in his hand when greeting a visitor?"

" Oh, that. Maybe he has reason to be careful."

" Maybe he has."

" What else did you think of him?"

" I think he is a very sick man."

" It's only the last year or so he's been like that. When we came here he was very different."

" I know," Cade said.

She had been moving restlessly about the room. Now she sat down facing Cade. " You know who he is, don't you?"

" Yes, I know who he is."

" I expect Harry told you."

" No, Harry didn't tell me. I didn't know until I saw him in there."

" You recognised him?"

" Yes. I saw quite a lot of him in Buenos Aires. I was working on a newspaper."

" Did he recognise you?"

" I don't know."

" You'd better hope he didn't."

" Why?"

" He's not as helpless as he looks, and he can be mean
as hell. He wouldn't want you to go spreading the
glad tidings that Carlos Rodriguez is holed up in Venezuela, would he?"

" I'll bear that in mind," Cade said.

She looked puzzled, a shade worried perhaps. " Look,
Robert, you said you were Harry's friend. Right?"

" Right."

" A close friend."

" You could say that."

" Then what I don't understand is why he didn't tell
you about Carlos."

" He didn't have a lot of time."

" Why not?"

Cade hesitated. He hated doing it; it was like hitting
somebody who could not hit back. And yet she had to
learn about it some time, and maybe it was best that she
should hear it now.

" There's something I've got to tell you, Della. Harry
is dead."

He thought she was going to faint. Her eyes went
wide and her jaw sagged. She swayed a little and she
looked sick, almost as sick as Gomara. She made little
gasping sounds as though she were trying to speak and
the words would not come. But at last she managed to
say : " It's not true. You're lying. I don't believe it. It
can't be."

" It is true, Della. I only wish it wasn't. But it is."

" Oh, God," she said. " How did it happen?"

" He was murdered."

" By those two?"

" What two?"

" Lopez and Guzman."

So she knew about them. It was to be expected that she would.

" Could have been. No absolute proof. They were still looking for the killers when I left England."

" I warned him. I told him to be careful."

" He was careful. That's why he came to see me."

" And a hell of a lot of good that did him." She sounded resentful, as though blaming Cade for what had happened. Then suddenly a thought seemed to come into her mind. " Hey," she said. " What did you mean by that?"

" By what?"

" What you said about him coming to you because he was being careful. You told me he asked you to bring me a message."

" That wasn't strictly true."

" No? Then why did he come to see you?"

" He wanted me to look after a parcel for him."

She seemed to stiffen. " A parcel?"

" That's right. Brown paper. Sealed up. About so big." He demonstrated with his hands.

There was a tenseness about her now. Her gaze was on Cade's face, searching.

" Did you open the parcel?"

" After Harry was killed it seemed the logical thing to do."

Her voice was so low that he could hardly catch the words; but he could have guessed the question anyway. " What was in it?"

"One hundred and forty thousand pounds' worth of diamonds," Cade said.

There was a long silence. Cade and the girl looked at each other. She had recovered from the shock and her colour had returned to normal. Whether she had been genuinely in love with Harry Banner or not, Cade was pretty sure that she was not the one to cry over him for long. In fact there was no suggestion of tears in Della Lindsay's eyes. She would be thinking about herself, figuring out how to cut her losses.

As if to confirm his suspicions, she said : "The diamonds are mine now. They all belong to me."

Cade smiled. "Now I wonder just how you'd set about trying to prove that to the judge in a court of law."

"Are you aiming to hold on to them?"

"For the present, yes."

She jumped up suddenly and slapped him on the cheek. "You damned thief. What right have you to them?"

She might have struck him again, but he gripped her wrists and held them. She was trembling with rage and there were tears in her eyes now; but they were not tears for Harry Banner; they were all for Della Lindsay.

"If it comes to that," Cade said, "I wonder just what right you have to them?"

"Let me go," she said, kicking at his shins.

"I will if you'll promise to be calm."

"What makes you think I'm not?" she asked, looking about as calm as a tornado. "Let me go."

He released her and she seemed to be in two minds whether to lash out at him again, but she probably came to the conclusion that in a contest of strength he had too much of the edge. She returned to her chair and sat there glowering at him and gnawing her lip.

"Before we go any further," Cade said, "I think you'd better tell me about Lopez and Guzman. In fact it'd be a good idea if you told me the whole story—right from the beginning."

She stared at him sullenly. "What is the beginning?"

"Well, let us say for argument when Harry turned up in San Borja."

"Why should I tell you anything?"

"I've got the diamonds, remember? You want them. If you play your cards right you might still get them—some of them anyway. Who knows?"

He was watching her carefully and he saw that the hint had gone home. She stopped glowering and looked at Cade with a calculating eye.

"Harry didn't tell you much then?"

"Very little. But I've found out that he came to San Borja with Lopez and Guzman. Then he got a job here. How did he work that?"

"I told you. He used the old Banner charm. You know what Harry was like. He could talk his way into anything."

"Maybe you helped him get the job."

"Well, maybe I did. I met up with him one day in San Borja. He was a fast worker."

"He knew who Gomara was of course?"

"He had a pretty good idea. He and those other two had traced him here; don't ask me how. But they couldn't be dead certain they'd got the right man until Harry saw him."

" What was their game—Lopez and Guzman?"

" The same as Harry's of course—money. They knew
Carlos had got away with plenty and they meant to
lever it out of him. Harry told me they were all for
making a raid on this place; that shows you what brains
they have. Harry said no; he said Carlos would have
more sense than to keep much in the house; he'd have it
stashed away somewhere. So then they suggested kid-
napping me and making Carlos cough up for my ransom.
That one really made Harry laugh; the idea of Carlos
Rodriguez handing out big money to get back a woman
was just too rich. It'd be a whole lot cheaper to let the
old one go and get a new one. Besides, the way he is now,
what does he want a woman for?"

" Are you asking me?" Cade said.

She ignored the question. The hem of her dress had
climbed up so high that Cade could see the lace trim-
ming on her briefs; they were pale blue in colour. She
pulled it down with an impatient tug of her hand.

" The next idea those bright boys came up with was
to kidnap Carlos himself. That way they thought they
would soon shake the shekels out of him."

" But Harry didn't like that either?"

" No. He said the easiest way of all was just to play
on Carlos's fears. Carlos knows there are plenty of people
in Argentina who'd give their ears to find him. And some
of them wouldn't be above using a knife or a gun if
they ever got near enough to him."

" So Harry took the job just to get near Gomara, so
that he could bring the pressure to bear? Is that it?"

" That's it. Funny in a way. There was Carlos thinking he'd got a good strong-arm man to keep the wolves

at bay, and all the time the strong-arm man was a wolf himself."

" Was José here then?"

" Yes. But Carlos never let José get as close to him as Harry. He really seemed to take to Harry—at first. It made José pretty mad. He'd been working for Carlos for years, and then Harry walks in and he's the blue-eyed boy in a couple of shakes. Living in the house while José had to be content with bedding down in the old vaqueros' quarters."

" Did they ever quarrel?"

" José and Harry? You bet your sweet life they did. But Harry was tough; he could look after himself."

" In the end he couldn't."

She gave a sigh that sounded genuine. " That's true."

" José looks tough too."

" He is. And mean. He's as mean as old boots. Well, he's got where he wanted to be. He's Carlos's right hand man now."

" How long was it before Harry showed his cards?"

" Two or three weeks. He was feeling out the ground."

" Making sure of you too?"

" Well, yes, I guess so. Lopez and Guzman were getting impatient. They wanted him to hurry things along. But he went at his own pace."

" Intending all the time to double-cross them."

Della shook her head. " Not at first. Only later, when he teamed up with me. He said there wouldn't be enough to go round and two would have to be unlucky."

" He was the unlucky one."

" Oh God," she said. " Do you have to remind me?"

"How did Gomara take it when Harry started to work on him?"

"How would you expect him to take it? He was mad as all hell. But he was scared too. He doesn't want to die. Though what he has to live for now, goodness knows."

"Why didn't he kill Harry? Or get José to kill him. I should think José would have done it."

"Sure he'd have done it. But Harry didn't give him the chance."

"How did the diamonds come into it?"

"Carlos had them in a bank in Caracas. He's got money in other places too of course, but Harry thought the diamonds would be just right—easy to shift, always saleable, never likely to go down in value."

"How did he know about them?"

"He didn't until I told him. That was my idea really. Carlos used to talk to me about them sometimes. He used to ask if I liked diamonds, and then he'd say that if I was a good girl and did exactly what he told me maybe some day I'd have them."

"You might have done better to wait for them to come to you that way."

"They never would have. It was just talk. I know because there were other times when he told me I'd get nothing when he died. That was a way of making sure of me. He said he was worth more to me alive than dead and I'd better remember it."

"So Harry went to Gomara and demanded the diamonds as payment for his silence?"

"Yes."

"And Gomara gave way—just like that?"

"Not at once. It took a bit of time. But, like I told you, he's scared. Harry knew the way to play on his fears and he was clever enough not to put the price too high. Carlos could afford that much and still be a rich man. Harry told him it was better to have a little less and be alive than keep it all and be dead. You can't take it with you."

"So I've heard," Cade said. "Who fetched the diamonds from Caracas?"

"I did. Carlos gave me written authorisation and I flew to Caracas and drew them out of the bank."

"You went alone?"

"Yes."

"Harry was very trusting. You could have taken off from there and never come back."

"Do you think I'm looking for trouble? I like to live."

"So you came back, gave the diamonds to Gomara and he handed them over to Harry?"

"That's right."

"Why didn't you leave with Harry?"

"He said better not. He said he'd let me know when and where to join him."

"It didn't occur to you that he might be double-crossing you too?"

She flared up again and seemed about to jump up from her chair and rush at Cade, but she decided against it. "That's a damned filthy suggestion," she said. "He wouldn't have done a thing like that. He loved me."

"All right," Cade said. "So maybe he did and maybe he wouldn't. It's an academic question now anyway. Do you think Gomara suspects you were in cahoots with Harry?"

" Oh God," she said, " I hope not. But sometimes I wonder. He has a way of looking at me that makes me think sometimes he has suspicions. Hell, I wish I could get away from here, but now—" She gave another sigh. She seemed depressed and uneasy.

Cade got up from his chair. Della stood up too.

" What are you going to do now?" she asked.

" I'm going back to my hotel."

" You know that isn't what I meant. What are you going to do about the diamonds?"

" I haven't decided."

She moved up close to him and he could smell the scent that she used; it was probably the kind that came in fancy bottles and cost the world. There was a little golden down on her upper lip and she had long eyelashes that could have been her own.

" You know half of them belong to me," she said, and there was a purring, seductive quality in her voice.

" Do I know that?"

" Of course, Robert." She put her hands on his arms and slid them up until they met behind his neck. " Of course."

Cade stood perfectly still. He felt her body moulding itself against his own and he felt the pressure of her hands pulling his head down towards her parted lips.

" We could make a team, Robert, you and me. A real good team."

Cade said nothing. He was reflecting that it had not taken Della long to transfer her favours, but he was not fool enough to believe there was anything personal in it : it was not his manly attraction she had fallen for but the pull of one hundred and forty thousand pounds' worth of sweet and lovely diamonds. There was a lot of sex-appeal in that amount of precious stone.

"Robert, darling."

Her mouth was very close. Cade put his arms round her and pulled it closer.

At that moment he heard a sound behind him. He released the girl and turned. Carlos Gomara was sitting in his wheelchair in the open doorway. He was smiling faintly, but it was not a pleasant smile.

"Ah, Señor Cade," he said in his whispering voice. "Forgive me for intruding. I was under the impression that you had gone."

"I am just leaving," Cade said. He walked to the table and picked up his jacket.

Gomara made a fluttering gesture with his hand. "No hurry. I can quite understand that you must have a great deal to say to Señorita Lindsay. Consider yourself free to come whenever you feel inclined to continue the—ah —conversation. Please look upon my house as your own."

There was an undertone of venom in the words, although Gomara continued to smile. If one of the snakes in the pit had spoken Cade felt that it might have used just such a voice. He wondered how long Gomara had been in the doorway and how much he had heard.

Della said, as though she felt compelled to offer some explanation: "Robert is an old friend."

Gomara looked at her and there was no longer a smile on his face. "An old friend. Is that so? How strange that you did not tell me so before. But no doubt you forgot. It is so easy to forget who one's friends are."

The girl stared at him for a moment, then shivered as though a chill had passed through her and turned away. She moved to a window and stood looking out, her back to the room.

"Thank you for your hospitality, Señor Gomara," Cade said. He walked past the wheelchair and into the hall. He opened the front door and let himself out of the house.

José was waiting at the gate. He unlocked it and swung it open. Cade drove slowly through.

"Please wait for a moment, señor," José said.

Cade stopped the Citroen just clear of the gateway. José closed the gate and walked to the car. Without a word he opened the nearside door and got in.

"What are you doing?" Cade demanded.

"You are going to San Borja, señor?"

"Yes."

"Then you will not refuse to take a passenger, eh?"

It seemed a strange way to ask for a lift into town, and José was certainly not the passenger that Cade would have chosen to accompany him, but there seemed no good reason for refusing so small a favour.

"You will have to make your own way back."

"I can do that."

"All right then," Cade said, and let in the clutch.

No other word was spoken until they were approaching the road junction. José sat upright on the seat, staring ahead, expressionless, his thin lips pressed together in a hard, straight line. He had a curved beak of a nose and prominent cheekbones. There was probably Indian blood in his veins.

They were about fifty yards from the junction when he spoke again. He said : " You will turn right at the other road."

" It is left to San Borja."

" Nevertheless, señor, you will turn right."

" That will take us to the mountains."

" Yes."

Cade looked at José and saw that there was a thin-bladed knife in his left hand. The point of the knife was some two inches from Cade's lowest rib.

" What is the game?" Cade asked.

" No game, señor. You will turn right."

" Suppose I refuse?"

" Then it will be the worse for you." As if to emphasise his argument he moved the knife a little way and Cade felt the sharp pricking of the steel through his shirt. " You understand?"

Cade understood. He understood only too well. It was obvious that while he had been having his talk with Della Lindsay Gomara had had a little talk with José. Gomara must have recognised him after all, or perhaps he was just playing safe.

There was one other possibility : Torres might have carried out his threat of warning Gomara. That might have been why Gomara had let him in, letting him walk into the trap. But Torres would have had to move very swiftly in getting the message through, so perhaps he was innocent in that respect. Either way, the result was the same.

At the junction he thought of turning left and to hell with it. The pressure of José's knife dissuaded him. He turned right.

NINE

A RIDE WITH JOSÉ

IT WAS the way Earl Johnson and Juanita Suarez had gone the previous day, the way to the mountains; a rough, stony road that became rougher and stonier the farther they went.

It was also a deserted road.

"Where are we going?" Cade asked.

"To the mountains, señor."

"For what purpose?"

"You will see."

Cade could make a pretty shrewd guess. What better situation as the setting for a neat piece of liquidation? There were many ways in which a man might lose his life up there in the hills and a lot of them could look like plain accident. He began to wish now that he had brought the revolver after all; a hell of a lot of good it was doing back at the Phoenix in his holdall.

He wondered whether it might be possible to bribe José, but a glance at the stern, sun-tanned face of the man beside him convinced him that he would be wasting his time to try anything in that line. He could not offer enough to tempt José from carrying out his master's orders.

So was there a possibility of overpowering him? A sudden twist of the wheel throwing him off balance, a swift blow to the head. He rejected that idea also. The knife was in José's hand; he had only to give one thrust and it would plunge to the hilt into Cade's side. José had nothing to lose; he could change places with the dead body and drive on.

" You have orders to kill me, perhaps?"

" My orders are no concern of yours," José said.

Cade could almost have laughed; the statement was so absurdly false. " On the contrary, they are very much my concern—in the circumstances."

José said : " You should not have come here, Señor Cade. Nobody asked you to come. Anything that happens to you, you will have brought on your own head."

" That will be a great consolation," Cade said.

The road began to wind. It snaked upward between tall outcrops of rock, stunted trees, scrub, boulders. They had come to the foothills and in front of them the mountains rose like an immense barrier, denying the right of anyone to pass.

They came on the jeep suddenly round a sharp bend. The jeep was standing back from the road in a space between two boulders and there was no one in it. Cade put his foot on the brake, but José immediately pressed the knife into his side.

" Drive on."

Cade drove on. As he passed the jeep he sounded the horn, but again José pressed the knife in under his ribs.

" Stop that."

Cade stopped it. There was no sign of Johnson. No sign of anyone. No help at all for a man driving to his own execution.

José seemed to relax a little. At least he stopped pressing the knife into Cade's flesh. Cade was glad of that; he was uncertain whether the dampness in that part of his shirt was being caused by sweat or by blood. Maybe a little of both.

" The jeep belongs to a friend of yours perhaps?" José said.

" Not friendly enough to be in it."

José laughed. It was the first time Cade had heard him laugh, and the sound was quite startling; it was like a dog yelping, strangely high-pitched. He stopped as suddenly as he had started and Cade hoped he would not do it again; it was bad for the nerves—other people's nerves.

About a mile farther on they came to some derelict mine workings.

" Turn left here and go slowly," José said.

The warning to go slowly was hardly necessary; no one but a maniac would have tried to drive fast on that kind of track. It led in between high walls of rock, sloping upward at first, then gently downward. As it went down it widened and Cade could see some old rusting railway lines and a few mine wagons, some tipped over on their sides, the wheels motionless, as they had been for years. There was some primitive machinery too, all dead and rusty and silent, just as it had been abandoned when the mine had become no longer profitable enough to be worked. There was something eerie about the place;

it was like coming on a skeleton, a grim reminder of the transience of all human activity.

"Stop here," José said. "Switch off the engine."

Cade obeyed. The knife was again touching his flesh.

"A pleasant view, señor," José remarked.

There was nothing very pleasant about it to Cade's way of thinking. The car was halted on a gentle downward incline, and about thirty yards farther on the ground fell away in a sheer drop where the rock appeared to have been quarried. From the car it was impossible to tell how deep the quarry was, but it was probably deep enough. A car falling over the edge was not likely to be of much more use. Nor a man in the car.

It was quite clear to Cade what José's intentions were : he meant to send the car with Cade in it crashing into the quarry. It would get rid of Cade once and for all and it would look like an accident. From José's point of view —and Gomara's also—what could be better? To Cade it looked less attractive; indeed, it looked so unattractive that he decided at once that if the car should go over the precipice he for one would not go with it.

The knife was still pressing into his side, but it was quite obvious that José could not remain there unless he was prepared to sacrifice his own life too; and that was really not on the cards; there must be limits to his devotion to his employer's interests. The conclusion was, therefore, that he intended getting out of the car before it took its final plunge; and when José got out what was to prevent Cade getting out too?

Cade sat and waited for José to make the next move. José seemed to be in no hurry to make it; perhaps he too had seen the problem, a problem that he had possibly overlooked until this moment. José was not, Cade judged, a very clever man, and it was apparent that he had not thought out his plan with sufficient attention to detail. He wished the tragedy to look like an accident; therefore he could not kill Cade with the knife because the body might be examined and the wound might be found. So what was he to do? It looked remarkably like stalemate.

"It is, as you remarked, a pleasant view," Cade said at last, "but it becomes a little monotonous after a time."

"You are tired of it already, señor?"

"I have to admit that I am."

"Then we will move," José said. And as he spoke he lifted the knife and struck Cade on the side of the head with the heavy bone handle.

Cade fell over to his left against the door. He was dazed but not completely unconscious. It was as though something had exploded inside his head like a small mine. He had difficulty in focusing his vision, even more difficulty in moving; the blow seemed to have paralysed him. His brain was working sluggishly; everything seemed veiled in a kind of mist; but through the mist he was dimly aware that José was releasing the handbrake and then that José was getting out of the car. The door slammed.

At first the car remained stationary; the slope was not steep enough to overcome the inertia of the vehicle. But after a moment or two it began to move, and in a detached kind of way Cade realised that José must be pushing it. He even wondered whether José would have to push it all the way to the precipice or whether, once started, it would roll forward under its own momentum.

And then it occurred to him that he ought to be doing something himself. Like pulling on the hand-brake or pressing down the pedal of the foot-brake. His sluggish brain worried at this choice of action for a while without coming to any decision. He could see through the windscreen, and he noticed that the edge of the quarry was coming slowly towards him. This strange phenomenon of a moving quarry puzzled him for a moment, until with a prodigious effort of reasoning he got the answer : it was not the quarry that was coming towards him but he that was approaching the quarry.

Again he thought of the brake, and he began feeling around with his right foot until it came on a pedal. He pressed the pedal, but it made no difference; the car still moved forward. It took him a few more precious moments to realise that he must have pressed the wrong pedal, and by that time the edge of the quarry was scarcely ten yards away and the car was gaining speed.

The immediacy of the danger served to clear the mists from his brain. He reached out and got his fingers on the hand-brake lever. He pulled it. The car's speed slackened but it did not come to a complete halt; it was still inching forward and it was now within a yard or two of the precipice. Cade searched again with his foot, and this time he found the right pedal. He stood on it and the car halted.

He felt sick and his head was buzzing like a swarm of bees. He looked out over the quarry and that did his sickness no good at all. He sat there and waited for José to come and finish the job with his knife.

He was still waiting when he heard a sharp, cracking sound. It was like a pistol-shot, but who would be firing a pistol up there in the mountains? Maybe his sense of hearing was playing tricks, and there was so much singing and buzzing going on inside his head that it would not have been at all unlikely.

Nevertheless, he turned his head to make sure. He turned it slowly in order not to upset the sensitive mechanism any more than it had already been upset, and then he saw that there really was a man with a pistol in his hand, and the man was Earl Johnson. A short distance farther back up the slope the jeep was standing.

José was about five paces from the back of the car. He had turned and was facing Johnson, the knife gripped in his right hand. There might have been twenty yards separating the two men, no more.

Johnson shouted something. It sounded like "Drop the knife." But José did not drop the knife. With a movement so swift the eye could scarcely follow it he lifted his hand and threw the knife at Johnson.

The knife-blade flashed in the sunlight as it sang through the air. Johnson swayed to one side like a bull-fighter avoiding the horns and the knife went past within an inch of his right shoulder. Then the sharp, cracking sound came again and a spurt of dust was kicked up at José's feet.

He began to run. He ran away from the quarry in the direction of the railway lines. Johnson yelled at him to stop but he paid no attention. Johnson fired again, again kicking up the dust near José's feet, but the only effect was to make him put on a little extra speed. A few seconds later he had disappeared into the opening of a tunnel that probably led to some of the abandoned mine workings.

Johnson put the gun away in his pocket and walked to the car. He peered in at Cade.

" You admiring the scenery, Rob?"

" José recommended it," Cade said.

" I wouldn't take his recommendation on a solid gold ring. Why don't you get out?"

Cade shook his head and regretted it. The brain cells seemed to swill round inside. " Not a chance. If I take my foot off the brake I'm afraid she'll move forward. There's a nasty drop just ahead—or hadn't you noticed?"

" No more than a hundred feet, I guess."

" Mr. Duero wouldn't like me to drop his car in there. He puts a high value on it."

" You aim to sit there for the rest of your life?"

" If I let the brake go there might not be much of my life left."

" I'll put rocks under the back wheels," Johnson said. Cade thanked him.

Johnson came round to the front again. " Okay; she's anchored now if you want to get out."

Cade took his foot off the brake very carefully. The Citroen did not move. He opened the door gently and stepped out. He walked away from the precipice and his legs felt like a couple of lengths of boiled spaghetti. He got as far as the jeep and leaned on it.

" You like to tell me what that guy has against you?" Johnson said.

Cade put two fingers to his head where José had hit him with the knife-handle. There was a swelling and a little blood, but it could have been worse.

" It's nothing personal. He was doing it for a friend."

" Would the friend's name be Carlos Gomara?"

" That's what he calls himself."

" You did him an injury?"

" Worse than that. I recognised him."

Johnson tapped his jaw. " As Carlos Rodriguez maybe?"

Cade looked at Johnson in surprise. " You knew?"

" Not for certain. I suspected it. I've been trying to get corroboration; that's why I wanted to see him, but I was headed off by the watchdog. You're dead sure Gomara is Rodriguez?"

" I'm sure," Cade said. " He's aged a lot, but I saw enough of him in Buenos Aires to know. Besides, Della Lindsay admitted it. And why should he want me pushed over a precipice if it were not true?"

" I guess you're right. It's not the sort of thing you do to every guest."

" Anyway, what's it to you? You're an oil man."

Johnson grinned. " I think it's about time you and me came clean, Rob. We seem to be overlapping. Suppose you tell me what your interest in Rodriguez is and then I'll tell you what mine is. Right?"

Cade thought this suggestion over for a while, then he said : " All right. I'm here because a friend of mine named Harry Banner was killed in a cheap hotel in London. He'd just come back from Venezuela. He told me he'd worked for a man named Gomara who had a place ten miles out of San Borja. I wanted to find out why he was killed and by whom. So I came and did a bit of nosing around."

" And have you found any light?"

" A little. Just a little."

He did not mention the diamonds. He saw no reason for telling Johnson all the details.

" Did Banner know Rodriguez too?" Johnson asked.

" Yes."

" Maybe he was trying to shake him down for a nice fat pay-off as the price of his silence and Rodriguez had him liquidated like he just tried to liquidate you."

" Maybe so," Cade said. " Now what's your interest in him?"

" I'm a private investigator. Portland Inquiry Agency, Philadelphia."

It explained the gun. It did not explain his interest in Gomara, but his next words did.

" I'm working for a syndicate in Argentina. I'm hired to find out where Rodriguez is holed up. I've been working on this case for six months. Elusive sort of guy, Mr. Rodriguez."

Elusive or not, other people who were not even private eyes had found him. But Cade did not tell Johnson this; it might have injured his self-esteem. Always supposing private eyes had any.

" What about the oil?"

" Smoke-screen," Johnson said. " You have to be something. Still, it's not been all wasted. I kick this geology stuff around for a hobby. Found some nice rocks up here. I was doing some chipping when you went past. Heard you hoot; wondered why the heck you didn't stop and decided to follow."

" I'm glad you did."

" Well," Johnson said, " I guess my job's about finished here now. All that remains is to tell the syndicate."

" You know what they'll do?"

" I'm not interested," Johnson said. " Look, I've got a rope in the jeep. Let's pull that jalopy away from the brink of disaster."

" Are you going to do anything about José?"

" To hell with José," Johnson said. " He never did anything for me except throw a knife at my guts. Let the bastard walk home."

TEN

VISITORS

MARTIN DUERO was still filing a piece of metal when Cade took the Citroen back. It could have been the same piece; it looked smaller. He seemed relieved to see the car. He waddled up to it, wiping his hands on an oily rag and sweating a little.

"No trouble, señor?"

"Not with the car," Cade said.

Duero looked at Cade's head. "Other trouble perhaps?"

"Something hit me when I wasn't looking."

Duero made sympathetic noises. "You have enemies, señor?"

"We all have enemies," Cade said. "I may want the car again tomorrow."

"It will be here," Duero said.

Señora Torres was deeply concerned. "You have been injured, Señor Cade. How did it happen?"

"An accident. Just an accident."

She raised her hands in horror. "You have had an accident with Martin Duero's car?"

"No, not with the car. I walked into something hard."

It was a close enough description of what had happened; José was certainly hard. He wondered whether José had made his way back to the Gomara place yet. It would be a long hot walk, and he was probably not used to walking. Cade drew quite a lot of pleasure from the mental picture of José with blisters on his feet. He had taken a lot from José; he was still feeling a little sick and his head was still aching as a result.

"You do not look well," Señora Torres said. "I will get you an ice-pack for your head and then you must go and lie down."

"I think I will," Cade said. "I'd like a long, cool drink too."

He went to his room and washed, and a little later Señora Torres appeared with some ice in a polythene bag and the long, cool drink.

"You must put this pack on the swelling," she said. "It will make it go down."

"Suppose it freezes my brains?"

"No, no, it will not do that. But of course you are joking." She gave him a playful slap which did things for his head that he would rather not have had done for it. "I will leave you now. You must be very quiet, señor, and later you will feel better."

"I won't make a sound," Cade promised.

When she had gone he drank the long, cool drink and felt a lot better. He kicked off his shoes and lay down on the bed with the ice-pack pressed to the swelling on his head. The throbbing was muted. He closed his eyes.

The tap on the door was no more than a formality. The door opened immediately and Jorge Torres came in. Cade opened his eyes and groaned. Torres walked to the foot of the bed and looked at Cade, smiling in a gloating sort of way. It seemed to be giving him a great deal of pleasure to see Cade in his present state of health.

" My wife tells me that you have had a small accident, señor."

Cade stared back at him bleakly. " So?"

" I have come to offer my sympathy."

" I don't need sympathy."

" No? Perhaps you need someone to take care of you. A bodyguard perhaps."

" What makes you think that?"

" I think so, señor, because I do not believe you have had an accident. I think you have been doing business with some person who does not like you; some person who might even wish to see you dead."

" You're crazy," Cade said.

Torres shook his head slowly from side to side and showed his fine white teeth under the black moustache. " Oh, no, not crazy. It is perhaps you, Señor Cade, who are a little crazy. Crazy to go visiting Señor Gomara without your gun."

" How do you know I have been visiting Señor Gomara?"

Torres lifted his plump shoulders the fraction of an inch. " One keeps one's ears open; one makes certain deductions. Where else would you go in a hired car?"

" And what makes you think I went without my gun?"

Torres slipped his right hand inside his jacket and

when he pulled it out again it was holding the .38 Colt.
"This makes me think so."

"Damn you," Cade said. "You've been at my luggage
again."

Torres admitted the fact without shame. "You are
very careless leaving the bag unlocked. There is no telling
who might walk in and steal things."

"I can tell who would."

An expression of shocked surprise came over Torres's
face. "Señor Cade, you cannot mean that you think I
stole this gun."

"How would you describe it?"

"I removed it for safety. As I said, anyone might have
come in while you were away."

"All right," Cade said. "So you took it for safety in
my absence. Now I'm not absent any more, so you can
give it back."

"Of course, señor, when the small formalities have
been attended to."

Cade sat up and took the ice-pack from his head.
"What formalities?"

"For services rendered," Torres said. "I am surely
entitled to some reward."

"So that's it. Just another hold-up."

"You may call it that if you wish."

Cade was becoming angry, and anger was bad for his
head. "Give me back my gun and then get to hell out
of here."

"No, señor." Torres's voice had hardened slightly; it
was no longer quite so urbane; and the revolver was
not being held so negligently; it was even being pointed
at Cade, and Torres's finger was resting on the trigger.

Perhaps Torres was remembering his humiliation of the previous evening and was taking some revenge. "No, I will not get to hell out of here. Not until you pay me one hundred bolivars."

Cade stared down the muzzle of the revolver. It had a nasty look about it when viewed from that angle.

"You may need a gun," Torres said softly. "Especially if you propose to visit Señor Gomara again. If you are wise you will pay me what I ask. It is a small sum to give in exchange for one's personal safety."

"Are you threatening me, Jorge?" Cade asked.

"Threatening you? What makes you think I would do a thing like that? You are a guest in my hotel."

"Señora Torres's hotel."

Torres frowned slightly. Obviously he did not wish to be reminded of that unpalatable truth. "It is the same thing. We are man and wife."

"I think you would find it difficult to convince the lady that it is the same thing."

"Let us forget the hotel," Torres said, and his face had darkened and there was an angry glint in his eye. "Are you going to pay me one hundred bolivars for this gun?"

"Yes," Cade said. "I'll pay you, Jorge."

Torres looked surprised and gratified. Perhaps he had expected that it would have been necessary to exert rather more pressure. He also looked a good deal happier.

"I see that you are a prudent man, señor."

Cade swung his legs over the side of the bed. He lowered his feet to the floor and stood up. The ice-pack was in his right hand and with his left hand he felt in his trousers pocket. Torres lowered the gun and moved towards him ready to take the money. Cade was still fumbling in his pocket. Torres came closer. Cade swung his right hand in an arc and struck Torres on the point of the jaw with the ice-pack.

Torres staggered back. Cade followed up quickly and grabbed Torres's right hand with both his own. He twisted the hand back until Torres, with a squeal of pain, dropped the revolver. Cade picked it up and dug the barrel into Torres's paunchy stomach. It seemed to go in quite a long way.

" Do you want me to blast your guts out?" Cade said. The way his head was behaving made him feel savage. The way Torres had tried to shake him down for another hundred bolivars and had actually threatened him with his own gun made him feel even more savage.

Torres froze rigid. His frightened eyes stared back at Cade and his lips trembled. " It was a joke. I swear to you it was only a joke. I meant no harm."

" That kind of joke doesn't appeal to my sense of humour. Perhaps I've been threatened once too often."

" I did not threaten."

" I know. You would never threaten a guest in your own hotel—even if it does belong to your wife."

But there was no satisfaction in taunting Jorge Torres, no satisfaction in pushing a revolver barrel into his fat belly. He was too flabby. Cade pulled the gun away and Torres breathed again.

" Get out," Cade said.

Torres went out of the room faster than he had come in. He seemed afraid that Cade might change his mind.

He was almost asleep when another gentle tap came on the door. He ignored it. To hell with it; to hell with the lot of them.

The door opened a little way; a head appeared in the opening. Silky black hair. Dark eyes. Rounded chin. A voice said very softly : " Roberto !"

Cade sat up so quickly that he thought for a moment he had left his head on the pillow.

" May I come in?" Juanita asked.

Cade ignored the protest in his head and swung his feet to the floor. " Yes, of course."

Juanita came in and closed the door gently behind her. She was wearing a patterned silk dress, buttoned down the front and pulled in at the waist with a red belt. It did things for her figure—or her figure did things for the dress; Cade could not decide which. Either way, she looked like a dream.

" I have come to see how you are, Roberto. I hear that you have had an accident."

" Only a very small accident. A bump on the head."

He began to get up, but she said quickly : " No, do not move, not for me. You should rest." She came to the bed and put a hand on his shoulder, exerting a gentle pressure.

Cade sat down again.

" How did it happen? Señora Torres says you walked into something hard."

" That's what I told her."

She gazed into his eyes. " That something hard would not perhaps have been a man?"

" Is that what you think, Juanita?"

" It is what I think, Roberto."

" What gives you ideas like that?"

" I do not think you would be so foolish as not to look where you were going. Also you would have to be walking very fast to get a bump on the head like that."

" Sometimes I do walk fast."

She moved to the window, looked out on to the Plaza, turned. " Did you see Señor Gomara?"

" Yes," Cade said, " I saw him."

" You had trouble with him perhaps?"

" Why should I have trouble with Gomara?"

" Why did you want to see him?"

" I thought I told you. I'm a journalist. I wanted an interview."

He wondered whether she had been talking to Johnson, whether Johnson had told her anything. It was unlikely. Private eyes kept information pretty much to themselves except when it was to their advantage to dish a little out.

" Is he so interesting?" Juanita said.

" He interests me."

" What is he like, this Gomara?"

" You are interested in him too?"

" Just curious about a man who shuts himself away and keeps people out."

Cade wondered whether to tell her who Gomara really was, but he decided not to. She had probably never heard of Rodriguez anyway.

He said : " Gomara is a sick man, white-haired; he goes about in an electric invalid chair."

He thought she seemed a shade disappointed. Perhaps

she had expected something more startling. "So," she said musingly. "So."

"I interviewed him in a room with no furniture; just a snake pit."

She looked surprised at that. "A snake pit?"

"A concrete pit in the floor, full of snakes. He said he liked them. Some people have strange tastes."

"Poisonous snakes?"

"Oh, yes. Very lethal, I'd say. To tell the truth, I thought him a bit like a serpent himself."

"Could it have been a serpent that struck at you, Roberto?"

She was being very shrewd in her guesses, Cade thought. He wondered again whether Johnson could have told her anything. How close was she to the American? Close enough to share secrets? Rather to his own surprise, he felt a stab of jealousy. He did not want them to be too close.

"Has Earl been talking to you?" he asked.

"About what?"

"About Gomara and me?"

She shook her head. "Does he know something?"

"Who knows what he knows?"

"You're being very mysterious," she said. "Are you going to see Gomara again?"

"I don't know."

He was not at all sure he wanted to visit the Gomara place again. The way he felt now, he would not be very sorry to forget the whole affair and leave San Borja at the first opportunity. After all, he had got what he had come for: he knew how Harry Banner had come by the diamonds and why he had been killed. He even knew who had killed him. So what more was there to do in San Borja? No need for him to worry about Gomara; when Earl Johnson reported to the Argentine syndicate it was as certain as tomorrow's sunrise that Gomara would be very thoroughly dealt with. True, there was the matter of José; he was still burned up by the treatment he had received from that thug. José had not only pricked him in the side a number of times— and the marks were still there as evidence; he had not only struck him on the head with a knife-handle; he had also pushed him to the brink of death. For those things he owed José something. But was it worth the trouble? Was it really worth the trouble?

" I don't think so," he said.

Juanita frowned slightly. " I was hoping that you would go and take me with you. I would like to see that snake pit. You have roused my curiosity."

" Why not go by yourself?"

" I would not be allowed in. I have tried."

" You think they'd let you in if you went with me?"

" I think so. I think you have some influence there."

" You could be over-rating that influence," Cade said.

There was another problem too that was exercising his mind, the problem of what to do with the diamonds. He could think of several alternatives; perhaps there were always several possible courses of action where diamonds were concerned. Number one : he could send them back to Gomara, the rightful owner. No doubt Gomara would be duly grateful—if by that time he was still alive. But when it came to the pinch, was Gomara the rightful owner anyway? It was a thousand to one that he had come into possession of the gems by somewhat questionable means to say the least; and all things considered, Cade felt that he hardly owed Gomara anything after what had happened at the derelict silver mine.

Cross off Gomara.

Give them to Della Lindsay as compensation for the loss of her lover? There was little doubt that Miss Lindsay would appreciate the gesture; little doubt too that she would draw ample consolation from possession of those glittering stones. She might even erect some kind of monument to the memory of Harry Banner—if she felt she could spare the money. But he did not think that was quite on either. He was not worried about Della's future; diamonds or no diamonds, she would fall on her feet; she was that type.

Cross her off too.

Hand them over to Superintendent Alletson of the C.I.D. then? With the explanation that their existence had slipped his mind until that moment. He could imagine what Alletson would have to say to that. And was there not some law about withholding information and obstructing the police in the performance of their duty? Alletson would most certainly, as the saying was, throw the book at him. Cade had no wish to have any books thrown at him.

Regretfully, therefore, cross Alletson off too.

From a purely selfish point of view the fourth alternative was the most attractive of all : keep the diamonds for himself. Yes, that certainly had attractions—one hundred and forty thousand pounds' worth of them in fact. It was, of course, not strictly legal, but it was nearly so. Gomara had given the diamonds to Harry Banner, admittedly under some duress; Harry had given them to him, if you stretched a point; therefore they were his. He did not even convince himself.

Cross off Robert Cade? Well, put a question-mark against his name. A big, big question-mark.

"Roberto," Juanita said in the kind of voice that would have melted tungsten steel.

Cade saw that she had left the window and walked round the end of the bed. She sat down beside him and his pulse quickened. She would have quickened the pulse of an Olympic runner.

"Roberto," she said again, and her hand was on his arm. " Take me to see Gomara."

Cade swallowed.

" Roberto," she said, and now the other hand was stroking his forehead; and it was a funny thing but the head seemed not to be aching any more. Perhaps Juanita had the healing touch.

He thought of the proprieties, which were things he was not in the habit of giving much thought to. " Look," he said. " Suppose Señora Torres comes in. What will she think?"

" Do you mind what Señora Torres thinks, Roberto?"

" No," he said. " To hell with Señora Torres."

To hell with the proprieties too.

She kissed him and he reflected that this was the second time that day that he had been kissed by someone who wanted to persuade him to do something. Maybe he looked a pushover for that sort of thing. Maybe he was.

And then they were not sitting on the bed any more; they were lying on it. And he wondered just what this was going to do for his head; but he was not worrying because the head felt fine. There was a fragrance about

Juanita that was a delight to the senses; perhaps they used that kind of scent in paradise.

"Roberto," she whispered; and he wondered why Roberto sounded so much better than Robert. Maybe that extra letter did something for the name, or maybe it was simply the way she said it.

"Roberto, darling, you will take me to see Gomara tomorrow?"

Her hair was all round his face. His defences were being overrun and he had no spirit of resistance in him. He was a pushover sure enough.

He had a feeling that he would be using Martin Duero's Citroen again.

ELEVEN

CADE TAKES A PERSUADER

HE TOOK the revolver from the holdall and loaded the cylinder with rounds. Torres had loaded it when he had had the gun, but Cade had emptied it after Torres had left in haste. Now it was loaded again.

For a while he debated with himself the question of where to carry it. Strictly speaking, he ought to have had a shoulder holster, but there would have been something rather too melodramatic about a shoulder holster, and the harness was probably uncomfortable too, besides looking more than a little conspicuous if you discarded your jacket. Even Johnson did not wear one, and he was a professional.

He tried sticking the gun in the belt of his trousers, but it seemed awkward there and he had a feeling that you could give yourself a nasty injury that way if the thing went off by accident. Not that a revolver was likely to go off by accident, but the feeling was there all the same.

In the end he decided to carry it in his jacket pocket. It was a lightweight jacket, but not with the gun in it;

the gun itself weighed maybe a couple of pounds and it made the jacket hang down on the right side as if he was carrying all his spare cash in the pocket.

He left the hotel and walked to Duero's garage. He watched Duero check the oil and the petrol and the pressure in the Citroen's tyres.

Duero said: "I found some scratches on the back, Señor Cade. I think you should be a little more careful perhaps."

Cade wondered how Duero identified new scratches. Perhaps he kept a chart so that he could check up.

"The roads are not good," Cade said.

If the scratches were on the back of the car they had probably been made by splinters of rock thrown up by the bullets from Johnson's gun when he shot at José's feet. But he did not think it necessary to tell Duero that; it might have made him nervous for the welfare of his car. Just as it would probably have made him nervous if he had known that the Citroen had been within an ace of rolling over the edge of a quarry.

"That is why you should be careful," Duero said.

Cade promised to be careful, and he drove the Citroen very carefully out of the garage because Duero was watching him.

Juanita must have been looking out for him. She came out of the hotel almost as soon as he stopped the car. He got out and held the door for her. She was wearing a white linen dress and a sun hat. She looked cool, elegant, self-assured. Cade did not attempt to disguise his admiration.

"You make the car look shabby. Come to think of it, you make me look shabby."

She smiled. "You do not regret agreeing to take me with you?"

"I regret nothing," Cade said.

Johnson came out of the hotel as they were about to move off. He walked to the car and looked in. "So you're going to pay Gomara another visit?"

"Juanita wants to meet him."

"You think you can arrange an interview?"

"No, but I can try."

"Roberto is very persuasive," Juanita said.

"Uh-huh," Johnson said. "Maybe he's taking a persuader." He glanced at the bulge in Cade's pocket. "My advice to you, Rob, is be careful."

"That's what Duero advised. He found some scratches on the car. I think he's been over it with a magnifying-glass."

"I wasn't thinking about the car," Johnson said. "Well, I'll be moving along. Got a cable to send off." He walked away.

They came out of the town on to the hot, stony road, and a great cloud of dust rose behind them and slowly drifted away, settling like a blight on the thin and tufty grass. The car smelled of hot oil and petrol and rubber; it overpowered the unobtrusive scent that the girl was using.

"What did Earl mean when he said you were taking a persuader?" Juanita asked.

"He could have meant you."

"No, he did not mean that."

"Who knows what he meant?"

They passed three cars on the road and two horsemen. Traffic seemed light in that part of the world. When

Cade turned the car on to the road down to the Gomara place they could see the big white house and the out-buildings with the high fence enclosing them.

" It looks like a prison settlement," Juanita said, and she sounded subdued, as if the very sight of the place had depressed her.

" Maybe Gomara is a prisoner—in a way."

" I don't see—"

" He never leaves the house."

" You think he's afraid to leave it?"

" Could be."

The gate was padlocked. There was no sign of any-one on the other side. Cade stopped the car and sounded the horn. No one came.

" Where is everyone?" Juanita said.

" I don't think Gomara keeps many servants," Cade said. " I've only seen José and an old Negro named Andres who looks after the snakes. Della Lindsay said there were a couple of women to do the cooking and cleaning."

" Someone should come to the gate."

The place seemed dead. Cade wondered whether José had returned the previous day. Could it be that, having failed to carry out his orders successfully, he had decided to seek his fortune elsewhere? Perhaps he had been afraid that Cade would report the attempted murder to the police.

" Sound the horn again," Juanita suggested.

Cade did so. Nothing happened. It was hot in the car with the sun beating down on it. In the stable on the right a horse whinnied.

" One more go," Cade said. He gave a long blast on

the horn and suddenly José appeared, running from the direction of the house.

José was waving his arms and shouting. When he got close enough they could hear what it was that he was shouting.

"Go away! Go away!"

Cade got out of the car and walked to the gate. José was still shouting. When he saw that it was Cade he stopped.

"You!" he said.

He seemed both angry and frightened. There was a wild, half-crazy look about him; he kept clenching and unclenching his right hand, as though gripping some invisible object and then releasing it again.

"Open the gate," Cade said.

José made no move to do so. He glared at Cade. "Go away. There is nothing for you here. Go away, I tell you."

"I wish to speak to Señor Gomara."

"He will not speak to you. I have orders."

"I wish also to see Señorita Lindsay."

José's voice rose in pitch. "You cannot see her. You cannot. You cannot come in. Go back to San Borja. You will get nothing here."

He turned his back on Cade and began to walk away from the gate. Cade pulled the revolver from his pocket.

"Stop!" he said.

José turned and saw the gun.

"Now come back here," Cade said.

José hesitated a moment, then walked slowly back to the gate. He was staring at the gun as though it fascinated him.

"Unlock the gate," Cade said.

Again José hesitated. Cade thumbed back the hammer of the revolver.

"Unlock the gate."

Still José did not move. He licked his lips.

"I shall count up to five," Cade said. "Then I shall shoot you in the leg."

He began to count. José waited until the count had reached four, then gave in. He took the key from his pocket, unfastened the padlock and swung the gate open.

Cade eased the hammer of the revolver forward and put the weapon back in his pocket. He went back to the car, got in and drove it through the gateway. José looked like a man in torment.

"I know now what Earl meant by persuader," Juanita said. "Would you really have shot him in the leg?"

"He would do worse than that to me."

"That is not an answer to the question."

"Does anyone know what he will do until it comes to the push? Maybe I would have shot him. Maybe I'd have enjoyed doing it."

He stopped the car in front of the house. The front door was standing wide open. He led the way up the steps of the portico and Juanita followed. There was a wrought-iron bell-pull on the right of the door; it was made in the shape of a bull's head. Cade gripped one on the horns and pulled downward. Somewhere a bell jangled; then there was silence. No one came.

"Let's go in," Cade said.

They went in. The house was silent except for the buzzing of flies. It was hot and silent and brooding.

"Why does no one come?" Juanita said. She seemed

uneasy. Cade sensed an unusual tenseness in her. Her breathing had quickened.

Cade called softly : " Della ! Della Lindsay !"

There was no answer.

" She could be out riding."

" Does she ride?"

" Yes," Cade said. " She was riding the first day I came here."

" How many horses do they keep?"

" I don't know."

" There was one in the stable. It whinnied."

Cade was thinking about José. José had come from the direction of the house. If he had been in the house what had he been doing? And why had he been in such a state of excitement? He had been like a man in a frenzy even before he had seen who it was at the gate. So what had made him like that? Was it something that had happened in the house? And if so, what? And why was it all so silent now?

" Roberto," Juanita said.

He looked at her. Her lips were parted and it was certain that she was breathing more rapidly than was normal. There was something about her eyes too—a kind of glitter. She was more controlled than José had been, but in a way there was a similarity; she too was possessed by some deep emotion, a strange excitement.

" What is it?" he asked.

She touched his arm and he could feel her hand shaking, but he knew that it was not with fear.

" Where is the room with the snake pit?"

The question surprised him. It disturbed him a little too. He could not understand why she should want to know that. It was surely not the snakes that she had come to see. Or was it? Was she also a lover of snakes, like Gomara?

" Why do you ask?"

" Tell me," she said, and her hand tightened on his arm with a strength that he would not have expected in her.

And then it occurred to him why she wished to know. She had come to see Gomara and it was in the snake room that he might be found. It was there that he, Cade, had been received by the man. Perhaps he was there now, dozing in his wheel-chair in the oppressive heat of that room.

" It's along there," he said, pointing. " At the end of that corridor. Come; I'll show you."

" No," she said. " I prefer to go by myself."

" Don't you want me to introduce you to Gomara?"

" I can introduce myself. He won't send me away."

Cade felt that that was true. Gomara—or Rodriguez— had always been attracted by a pretty woman; even now it was unlikely that his tastes had changed entirely.

He told her which door it was and watched her walk down the corridor. He saw her open the door and go into the snake room. The door closed silently.

But he still did not know where Della was. Again he wondered whether she had gone riding. It was possible, yet he had a feeling that she had not. There was the horse in the stable. And there was still the nagging question of why José had come running from the house with that wild look in his eye.

Cade decided to make sure.

He looked first in the drawing-room where he had talked to her and where Gomara had found them together. There was no one in the drawing-room. He tried another room. There was a grand piano, a Turkey carpet on the floor, armchairs trimmed with gold braid, a number of oil paintings on the walls. No one was playing the piano; no one was looking at the paintings; no one was sitting in the armchairs.

Another room appeared to be a study. No one was studying.

He did not try the back of the house; he did not think she would be in the kitchens. He walked to the foot of the wide, curving staircase and began to climb the stairs. The staircase ended in a balcony with a mahogany balustrade and some mounted bulls' heads hanging on the wall. Cade guessed that they had been there before Gomara's time and that he had not bothered to get rid of them.

A passage led off from the balcony, doors opened from it to bedrooms. As soon as he entered the passage Cade noticed that one door was standing ajar.

He called again softly : " Della ! Are you there?"

No one answered. He pushed the door more fully open and walked in.

It was a large room, smelling of cosmetics and women's clothing. The pile of the carpet on the floor was so thick that it seemed to come up over his shoes like foam. There was a kidney-shaped dressing-table with big oval mirrors and so many jars and bottles it might have been the counter of a chemist's shop. Along one wall was a vast wardrobe with sliding doors, partly open, as though someone had been choosing a dress to wear. It could have been a difficult task; there were a lot to choose from.

He would have known it was Della's room even if she had not been there. But she was there. She was lying on the bed and she was wearing nothing but a pair of pale yellow briefs and a yellow brassière.

She did not get up when Cade walked in. She did not even look at him. It might have been supposed that she was asleep if her eyes had not been open. But there was something else that proved that she was not sleeping; for no one went to sleep with the handle of a knife protruding from the body just a little below the left breast. Or if they did, it was the kind of sleep from which there was no awakening in this world.

Della Lindsay would not be needing any diamonds where she had gone.

TWELVE

THE STABLE

CADE STOOD there utterly motionless, looking down at the lovely, useless body of Della Lindsay. There was some blood, but not a great deal. One cruel thrust of that cold steel blade had been enough to stop the pumping of her heart for ever. Nor did it take any great powers of deduction to guess who had pushed the blade in. No wonder José had had that wild look in his eyes when he had come running from the house.

But why had he killed the girl? Was this the paying off of some private grudge? Cade did not think so. He had a shrewd suspicion that in killing Della José had merely been carrying out orders, just as he had been carrying out orders when he had tried to send Cade to his death over the precipice. Behind it all was the sinister hand of Gomara. Gomara had heard too much of what had passed between Cade and Della; he had discovered the girl's treachery towards him and had taken his revenge—through José.

Cade suddenly began to move again. It was no use standing there; he had to find José. He felt a burning

anger against the man that was even hotter than the
anger he had felt when José had made the attempt on
his own life. Della had been amoral, fickle and dishonest,
but she had not deserved this; not a knife in the heart.
José had got to pay for what he had done; by God he
had got to pay. Gomara too. But Gomara could wait.
First it was José who had to be found.

He went out of the room and down the wide staircase and out of the house. The sun was hot; it spilled a
harsh, bright light over the house and outbuildings; it
wounded the eyes with its brassy spears. Cade stood on
the portico steps and looked for José. He could not see
him.

Then he caught sight of the old Negro who looked
after the snakes. Andres was coming round the corner of
the house. He looked startled when he saw Cade.

" Hey, you," Cade shouted. " Have you seen José?"

The old man shook his head. " I see no one, no one at
all."

He turned and went back round the corner of the
house like a rabbit bolting into its hole.

Cade thought of following him, abandoned the idea
as useless and began to walk towards the gate. The gate
was still open. José was not there.

Cade had almost reached the gate when he heard the
car. He glanced back and saw the Mercedes in which
Della had driven him back to San Borja. It had a different driver this time : José was at the wheel.

So José had decided that it was time to make a run
for it. The arrival of Cade and Juanita before he had
had time to dispose of Della Lindsay's body must have
upset his plans and sent him into a panic. Now he had

obviously come to the conclusion that he had better get out—and fast.

He was accelerating down the drive when Cade made a dash for the gate. It took him perhaps a second to get there and swing the gate across the path of the car. It was not the kind of gate you could drive straight through, not unless you were piloting a tank. José realised this and stood on the brakes. He was just a little too late. There was a screech of tyres, a cloud of choking dust, and the Mercedes hit the gate.

A lesser car might have crumpled. The Mercedes withstood the shock, the gate bent slightly and José was flung forward against the wheel.

But he recovered in a moment and was out of the car while Cade was still tugging at the revolver in his pocket. By the time he had got it clear José had disappeared inside the stable.

Cade went after him, the revolver in his right hand. There was a tall barn type of doorway in the end of the stable and it was through this that José had gone. The main door was shut but there was a wicket standing open and Cade went in by the wicket, stepping warily in case José should be lying in wait for him.

After the brilliant sunlight outside, the stable seemed gloomy. Cade's nostrils caught the sharp, ammoniacal tang of horse dung mingled with the scent of hay. There was also the unmistakable odour of leather harness, and he could see some saddles and bridles hanging near the door. The stable was divided down the middle by a kind of working alleyway. On the right was a hay loft and under it were some bales of straw, corn bins, sacks, a work-bench and various implements, most of them rusty and obviously seldom used. On the left was a row of loose-boxes, only one of which appeared to be occupied—by the black horse that Della had been riding when he had first seen her.

He could not see José.

He stood by the door, searching the stable with his eyes. There were scores of places where José could have been hiding and the task of ferreting him out was not an attractive one; it was about as pleasant a prospect as going into the lair of a wounded tiger. In fact, when you came to think of it, José was himself a wild animal and as dangerous as any that walked on four feet. Maybe more dangerous.

Cade shouted : " Come out José. You can't escape. You may as well give yourself up."

There was no answer, but the horse whinnied and stamped its hoofs. Cade could see its head over the door of the loose-box; it was looking at him, mutely questioning. It had a diamond blaze showing up whitely between the eyes.

He shouted again : " I'm coming for you, José. Make one false move and I'll shoot you."

He heard a faint hissing sound, felt something flick his ear as though a wasp had stung it, and heard a thud behind him. He turned and saw a knife imbedded in the timber of the door. José appeared to be well supplied with knives and he was certainly an expert in using them.

Cade stepped swiftly away from the door. He wondered where the knife had come from. He had seen no movement to betray the thrower; there had just been that faint hiss, the stinging of his ear and then the thud as the point had buried itself in the woodwork.

The horse moved again in its loose-box; it seemed to be nervous, too. José could see him and he could not see José. How many more knives had the man got?

It occurred to him that José might be hiding in one of the empty loose-boxes; perhaps that was one reason why the horse was nervous. The horse was in the nearest box. Cade did not think José would be in that one. He ducked below the level of the loose-box doors and crept past the horse, which shied back a little. He came to the next box and peered cautiously over the door. There was a scattering of straw on the floor, a drain in the centre and a manger at the far end. The manger was empty. So was the box.

He ducked down again and was creeping towards the next box when he heard a sound above him and on his right, a kind of rustling sound. He looked up just in time to see a baulk of timber hurtling through the air towards him. He dived forward and the baulk struck the door of the loose-box in which the horse was stabled, half-smashing the bolt holding it shut. The horse reared up and neighed, its eyes rolling in terror.

Cade knew where José was now. The baulk of timber had come from the loft. The loft was entirely open on the inner side; it was a large shelf with the hay piled on it, and there was a rough ladder at one end which José must have climbed immediately he entered the building. To get him Cade would have to climb it too.

He thought about it. And the more he thought about it, the less he liked it. There was really no reason, he told himself, why he should go up there after José. It was police work. Why not, therefore, go back to San

Borja and inform the police that there had been a murder at the Gomara place and that the murderer was holed up in a hay loft? Though, of course, by the time the police arrived he was not likely to be in the hay loft; he was more likely to be miles away and still moving.

Well, so what if he were miles away? Why should he, Cade, worry? It was not his duty to bring José to justice, not his duty to climb that ladder and tackle a man who was about as deadly as a jungle puma. Why should he not walk straight out of the stable and leave José to it?

But he knew the reason why he could not do that. It was lying on a bed in an upstairs room in the house; it was lying there very still with only a little blood on it; lying there open-eyed, but seeing nothing, hearing nothing, feeling nothing; lying there so close to the dresses it would never wear, the cosmetics it would never use; lying there waiting for the men to come and put it in a box and take it away and bury it in the ground.

A good enough reason.

He looked up at the loft. The light was poorer up there. He could see some hay piled up unevenly, but he could not see José. He could not hear him either. José was lying low, not moving, just waiting for Cade to come up the ladder.

Cade looked at the ladder. It went up almost vertically, so that he would need to use at least one hand in going up. It was the kind of ladder you could fall off very easily—even without being pushed.

The horse had calmed down a little; it came to the door of the loose-box and looked at him. But it was still nervous, and when he started to walk towards the ladder it backed away. He reached the ladder in five quick strides. He began to climb.

He was sweating now; the sweat ran down his face and he could feel his shirt sticking to him. He kept his right hand free while he climbed; the right hand was the one that held the .38 Colt. His hands were sweating too and affecting his grip on the butt of the gun, but he had to be ready to shoot at once if José appeared at the top of the ladder; he had to shoot before José could throw anything down on him.

He was half-way up when he heard the rustle of hay in the loft. He guessed that José was creeping towards the ladder and he did not wait; he started to fire the revolver. The horse neighed again and moved round in the loose-box, frightened by the sound, but the shots must have kept José back, for he did not appear at the ladder-top and in another moment Cade had climbed the last few rungs and had flung himself forward on the floor of the loft.

José was there sure enough. He was standing a few paces back from the edge with a pitchfork gripped in both hands. As Cade came off the ladder José lunged forward and downward.

Cade saw the pitchfork coming and instinctively rolled to one side. The tines of the fork straddled his left arm; he felt one of them graze his flesh as it pierced the sleeves of jacket and shirt, pinning them to the boards. The pressure of his finger on the trigger of the revolver was a kind of reflex action; he did not consciously take aim and the bullet went wide. José wrenched the pitchfork out of the floor and raised it for another thrust, but Cade was up on his feet in a moment and dodged in under José's lunge. The pitchfork passed over his head, and his shoulder took José in the stomach. José gave a grunt as the air was forced out of him and he went over backwards into the hay, still gripping the pitchfork.

Cade rammed the muzzle of the revolver into the base of José's ribs. " Drop it or I'll blow a hole clean through you. Drop it."

José stopped struggling. He dropped the pitchfork and it fell with a clatter to the floor of the loft. His face was close to Cade's and he was breathing heavily; his breath stank of garlic and strong tobacco; his body stank of sweat and unwashed linen.

" You damned murdering swine," Cade said. " Why did you kill her? What had she ever done to you?"

José sneered. " That whore. She deserved to die."

" You too," Cade said, and he ground the revolver into José's ribs. " Suppose I kill you now and save the law a job."

" And Señor Gomara. Will you kill him also?"

Cade stared into José's eyes. He saw no fear there; hatred, yes, but not fear. " Did Gomara tell you to kill the girl?"

" Who else? It was no concern of mine."

He was a cold-blooded bastard, Cade thought. He could drive a knife into a girl's heart and think no more of it than as a task that had to be done. Cade almost shot him then; his finger pressed on the trigger. José would never know how close he came to death in that moment. Or perhaps he guessed it, for he smiled crookedly, mockingly, despising the lack of ruthlessness that had saved him.

" Get up," Cade said.

José got up.

"Turn round and go down the ladder. If you try to run I'll shoot you in the back."

"You are a marksman, señor?"

"I shall not miss you."

José turned and walked to the ladder. He went down facing the rungs. Cade followed closely, gun in hand.

As soon as José's feet touched the ground he made a break for the door. Cade, still on the ladder, had to twist his body in order to aim the gun at him. It was an awkward position and he missed. The bullet flicked the horse instead, ploughing a shallow groove through the flesh of its haunch. The report of the gun combined with the sharp lash of the bullet sent the already nervous horse into a frenzy. The bolt of the loose-box door, weakened by the baulk of timber, gave way under the sudden pressure of the frightened animal and the door burst open just as José drew level with it. It struck him in the side and sent him reeling. He lost his footing and fell full length on the floor.

The horse came out of the loose-box as though the devil were driving it. Its hoofs clattered on the hard floor, came down on José's head, smashed it to a pulp and were gone. José's body twitched convulsively and then was still.

The horse had been Della Lindsay's. It had avenged her death.

Cade put the revolver back in his pocket and stepped down off the ladder. The horse had managed to squeeze through the wicket and had galloped off. Cade looked at José's dead body and turned away; it was not a pleasant sight. He followed the horse out of the stable and

walked towards the house through the brilliant sunlight.

He caught a glimpse of the old Negro and a couple
of women standing in a little group and looking in the
direction of the stable. They had probably heard the
sound of the shooting and had come from the back of
the house to see what was going on. As soon as they
saw Cade they hurried away and disappeared from view.
They all looked scared. Perhaps they had already been
scared when he had arrived with Juanita. Perhaps that
was why they had not answered the door-bell. He wondered whether they had known of Della's death.

Cade walked up the steps and into the house. He went
straight to the snake room, pushed open the door and
walked in.

Juanita was still there. She was standing perfectly
rigid with her back pressed hard against the right hand
wall and staring in front of her as though petrified.

Cade spoke to her. " Juanita."

She did not move, did not look at him. She might
not have heard.

He followed the direction of her fixed, unwavering
gaze and noticed for the first time what she was staring
at. It was something in the snake pit. He walked to the
edge of the pit and looked down.

One of the wheels was buckled and the chair was
lying on its side half in one of the shallow pools. Gomara
seemed to be curiously twisted; the back of his head was
in the pool but the water did not quite cover his face.
His mouth was open, and one might have imagined that
he was crying out in terror or agony, except that there
was no sound coming from his lips. There were no snakes

near him, but Cade could see some of them moving sinuously not far away.

How long, he wondered, had Gomara been in the pit? That he was dead was certain; but from what cause had he died? From the fall, from snake venom, or from something else?

He turned his back on the pit and went to Juanita. He saw now what he had not noticed before : in her right hand, which was hanging down by her side, she was holding a small automatic pistol. It had probably been in her handbag. The handbag was lying on the floor.

" You'd better give that to me," Cade said.

Again it was as though she had not heard. He took her hand and eased the gun from her fingers. She made no resistance.

He lifted the gun to his nose and sniffed. Nothing. He took the magazine from the butt and examined it. It was full. The gun had not been fired. He dropped it into the left-hand pocket of his jacket.

" What happened?" he asked.

She did not answer. He gripped her shoulders and shook her. " Juanita ! Answer me. What happened?"

It was like someone waking from a deep sleep, a dream, a nightmare perhaps. Her eyes gradually lost their fixed stare and her body its rigidity. She looked at Cade as if only then becoming aware of his presence.

" Roberto !"

" What happened, Juanita?" he repeated.

She shuddered. " I meant to kill him. That is why I came."

" That is why you brought the gun?"

"Yes." She looked at her right hand. "It's gone. Where is it?"

"I've got it," Cade said. "But you didn't kill him. The gun hasn't been fired. So what happened?"

She was becoming calmer. She frowned slightly, as though trying to marshal her thoughts.

"He was afraid. When I told him who I was and why I had come he was afraid. When I pointed the pistol at him he tried to get away. He turned the chair; one wheel went over the edge; he tried to save himself but could not. He fell in. The snakes. Oh, God, the snakes."

She lifted a hand to her eyes as though to shut out some horrible sight. Cade put his arm round her shoulders and waited for her to recover.

Then he said: "Why should he have been afraid when you told him who you were?"

"I recognised him. I had traced him here but I could not be certain until I saw him. Then I knew. You know who he was, don't you?"

"Carlos Rodriguez."

"Yes. Carlos Rodriguez."

"But why—"

"There was a girl who was found dead in Rodriguez's swimming-pool. A girl he had seduced, corrupted, killed. A girl only eighteen years old."

"Isabella Martinez."

"She was my half-sister."

THIRTEEN

NO MYSTERY

NICHOLAS MARCOS CLAVIGERO of the San Borja police was a large plump man with a gentle, slightly wheezing voice and somewhat protruding ears. He had a dark, smoothly-shaven face with eyes set so widely apart and so poorly aligned that it seemed not at all improbable that he might have been capable of seeing in two directions at once. And that, for a police officer, might have been a very useful ability.

"There are then, Señor Cade, three dead people at the house of Señor Gomara?"

"Yes," Cade said.

Clavigero sighed. He had a comfortable office with two electric fans which stirred the air even if they did not cool it very much. It was apparent to Cade that if he had been at all able to justify such an action he would undoubtedly have despatched some subordinate to investigate the matter. But three bodies—that was rather too many. He sighed again and lifted his heavy bulk from the chair in which it had been seated. He was sweating gently in spite of the fans.

"We will go to the house of the unfortunate Señor Gomara?" he said. "You, Señor Cade, will please accompany me."

The Citroen was standing in the shade of some trees outside the police-station, a square concrete building with a flat roof and white walls. Cade had already taken Juanita Suarez back to the Phoenix and had left her in the care of Señora Torres. He had told the Señora that Juanita was not feeling well and the Señora had promised to look after her.

"You must go and lie down, señorita. I will bring an aspirin and a cooling drink. It is the heat no doubt. So very hot it is."

Juanita thanked her. Cade believed she was still suffering from the shock of Gomara's peculiarly unpleasant death. He had told her nothing about Della and José. Time for that later.

"We will go in the police car," Clavigero said. "No need for you to waste petrol, Señor Cade. On the way we will go over your story again—in detail."

The police car was a big Ford, not very new, rather beaten up, like a suspect after questioning. Clavigero and Cade sat in the back and a sergeant sat in the front with the driver. The sergeant was a silent, morose sort of man with extraordinarily large hands and feet. The driver looked about fifteen years old, but that seemed hardly probable.

Cade went over the story in detail.

"You are an Englishman, Señor Cade?" Clavigero said.

"It is on the passport."

"Yes. So it is. I was merely stressing the fact. So,

as an Englishman, what are you doing in San Borja?"

"I am a journalist. I am writing a story."

Clavigero chuckled softly. "You will have plenty of material, it seems."

"That is not the kind of story I write."

"So?" Clavigero seemed a trifle disappointed. He had perhaps been anticipating world-wide press coverage of the crime with his own name in the headlines. "And what were you doing at Señor Gomara's?"

"I had an interview with him yesterday. He invited me to come again."

"And Señorita Suarez?"

"I invited her to accompany me."

"I shall of course need to question her later."

"Of course."

"And you did not, Señor Cade, in fact speak to Señor Gomara today?"

"No. When I saw him he was already dead."

"But Señorita Suarez spoke to him?"

"Yes. It was while she was with him that he accidentally fell into the snake pit with his wheeled chair."

"Accidentally," Clavigero said. "Yes, of course." He sighed. "Accidents will happen."

The Mercedes was standing a short distance back from the gate. Cade had had to move it before he could open the gate to let the Citroen through. The gate was still open; there were no enemies for Gomara to keep out now.

Clavigero told the driver to stop by the stable. "We will look first at this man José Rivera."

It was the first time Cade had heard José's surname.

He supposed Clavigero would make it his business to know a thing like that.

Cade went first through the wicket, then Clavigero, then the sergeant. The driver stayed in the car. There were flies on José's head. The knife was still sticking in the door, the baulk of timber that had broken the bolt of the loose-box was lying where it had fallen, but the horse had not returned.

Clavigero wheezed and sweated a little. He looked at José; he looked at the loose-box and at the knife; he looked up at the loft.

" Yes," he said. " Yes, I see."

There were dark stains on the floor where the horse's hoofs had carried some of José's blood. The sergeant pointed them out gloomily.

" I have seen them," Clavigero said. He looked at Cade. " You are fortunate to be alive, señor. That beam, that knife, either might have killed you."

" I know," Cade said.

" This Rivera was a very violent man. Perhaps it is fitting that he should have come to a violent end."

" He was certainly violent."

" Let us go to the house," Clavigero said.

The front door was closed. Cade had closed it before leaving. He had found the old Negro and the other servants and had told them to let no one in until the police arrived. Not that there was likely to be anyone to let in. They had all seemed stunned; he was not sure that they had understood what he had been saying.

Clavigero did not trouble to ring the bell. He opened the door and walked in. The others followed.

"I will look now at the woman," Clavigero said.

They climbed the stairs. They went into the room where Della was lying on the bed. The sergeant looked at her and seemed more morose than ever.

Clavigero sighed again. "Yes, I see. And this was exactly as you found her?"

"Yes," Cade said.

"Why did you come to Señorita Lindsay's bedroom?"

"I had looked in the other rooms."

"You were searching for her?"

"Yes."

"Why?"

"I wished to speak to her."

Clavigero gazed at the girl's face. "That is understandable. She was very attractive. Such a pity. It is always a tragedy when the young and beautiful die. There can never be too much beauty in the world."

When they went into the snake room Clavigero sweated even more. He took out a handkerchief and dabbed his face and chin. He walked to the edge of the pit and looked down at Gomara.

"We shall have to get him out of there."

"There are snakes," the sergeant said. He seemed afraid that Clavigero might order him to go down and lift Gomara out. "Venomous snakes."

"Nevertheless, the body cannot be allowed to remain there. That is out of the question."

"Andres would do it," Cade suggested. "He has a way with snakes."

Clavigero nodded to the sergeant. "Go and fetch the old man."

The sergeant went away.

Clavigero said : " There is no mystery here, I think. It is quite evident to me that the killing of Señorita Lindsay was a crime of passion."

" You think so?"

" I am certain of it. I have dealt with such affairs before. The woman was Señor Gomara's mistress. José desires her. It is natural; he is a man. She spurns him, laughs in his face perhaps. He is a servant, a menial, and she will have nothing to do with such a fellow. He goes to her room, consumed by desire. She is as we saw her, choosing a dress perhaps. The sight of her thus inflames him. He tries to embrace her. She resists, smacks his face perhaps, calls him names. In a fit of uncontrollable rage and jealousy he draws his knife and stabs her. He hears your car horn and runs out of the house, hoping to send you away until he can dispose of the body. You insist on being allowed to come in." Clavigero paused and looked hard at Cade. " That is one point that puzzles me. Why did he let you in?"

" I persuaded him," Cade said. " He was reluctant, but Señor Gomara had given orders that I was to be admitted at any time. And José could not have expected that I would go to the bedroom."

He had not told Clavigero about the revolver. That was one detail he felt it unnecessary to reveal. He had not mentioned Juanita's small automatic either.

" I see," Clavigero said. " Yes, that seems all perfectly clear. We shall, of course, test the knife for fingerprints. You did not touch it?"

" No."

" Then I feel certain that we shall find only José Rivera's prints on it."

He seemed highly pleased with himself. Perhaps it gave him a sense of achievement to have cleared everything up so quickly and efficiently. It would be a credit to the San Borja police department.

" And Señor Gomara?" Cade asked.

Clavigero shrugged. " An accident, as you said. An invalid in a wheel-chair; such men should not have snake pits without walls round them. Sooner or later it was bound to happen."

When he got back to the hotel Cade went straight up to Juanita's room. He knocked gently on the door and heard her voice, a little startled, it seemed.

" Who is there?"

" Robert. May I come in?"

She opened the door herself. She was obviously glad to see him, but she looked tired, as though the events of the day had drained the vitality from her.

" Roberto."

He closed the door and kissed her. " It's all right," he said. " The police are accepting Gomara's death as an accident. There'll be no trouble. I'm afraid you'll have to answer a few questions."

She looked worried. " Questions?"

" They'll want your version of what happened. Just tell them you were talking to Gomara and he accidentally sent the chair over the edge. That is what happened."

" Yes. That is what happened."

" Don't say anything about your gun. Or mine."

"I won't," she said.

"And there's something else you'd better know; something that happened out there."

She seemed to brace herself. "What else happened?"

He told her about Della and José.

"Oh God," she said. "You might have been killed."

"But I wasn't."

"Promise me you'll never do that again."

"Do what again?"

"Go chasing a murderer."

"It's not something I make a habit of doing," Cade said.

Earl Johnson was in the lounge when Cade went down. Johnson ordered drinks and piloted Cade to a seat where they would not be overheard.

"Some very strange rumours are floating around," Johnson said. "Maybe you know something about them."

"What kind of rumours?"

"That Gomara is dead for example. That Della Lindsay and José are also dead. That you and Juanita are rather deeply involved."

"Innocently involved," Cade said.

"Naturally. Like to tell me about it?"

"I don't know whether I should."

"I saved your life, Rob."

Cade told him.

Johnson thought it over. "I don't think my clients are going to like this very much. I kinda got the impression they wanted him alive. They wanted to deal with him themselves in their own way."

"We can't all get what we want."

"That's true. And they can't blame me. I didn't kill the guy."

"Nobody killed him. He was bitten by a snake."

"That's also true. And he had it coming to him. If anyone deserved to be snake-bitten he did."

"You'll be pulling out now, I suppose?"

Johnson nodded. "Nothing more for me here now."

"Nor me," Cade said.

"Let's drink to that."

They drank.

FOURTEEN

A SMALL FAVOUR

THE CUSTOMS officer at London Airport examined Cade's luggage with particular care. At least, so it seemed to him. He was glad he had ditched the revolver before leaving San Borja. True, he might well have a need for something of the kind even in England, but a gun was not the sort of thing that was easy to explain away to an eagle-eyed customs officer.

Cade had nothing incriminating in his luggage and he was passed through.

London looked cold and dreary and uninviting. In the blistering heat of Venezuela he had thought of this city with a certain nostalgia; now that he was back he found it less attractive. There was no one in London he really wanted to see.

There were, nevertheless, people he would have to see. Alletson for one. He rang up the superintendent as soon as he got back to the flat. As luck would have it, Alletson was in his office.

"This is Robert Cade speaking. I thought you'd be pleased to know I'm back in England."

"Why should I be pleased about a thing like that?" Alletson sounded dissatisfied with life. Perhaps the villains were getting him down. Or it could have been the weather.

"No reason at all," Cade said. "But you'd have cursed me if I hadn't let you know."

"You're right there. I want to talk with you. When can you get round here?"

"I'll have a shower to remove the grime of travel and then I'll be right with you."

Alletson's face looked to Cade just a little squarer and paler than it had been when he had last seen it. He was sitting at a desk littered with manila folders when a young constable showed Cade in. He waved a hand in the general direction of a chair.

"Sit down, Mr. Cade."

Cade sat down.

"Like a cup of tea?"

"Is it good tea?" Cade asked.

"It's lousy."

"I don't think I'll trouble then."

Alletson grunted. He opened a folder, looked at the papers inside and seemed to be depressed by what he saw. He sighed. It was not such a wheezy sigh as Clavigero's but he was not so fat. Perhaps sighing was an occupational disease of police officers.

"Have you caught those boys who killed Harry Banner?" Cade asked.

Alletson's reaction appeared to indicate that it was not the most tactful of questions. He looked sour. "If I had a bit more information to go on, and if certain

people who might be expected to help didn't go galli-
vanting off to distant parts of the world, I might stand
more chance of laying my hands on them."

Cade gathered from this rather lengthy answer that
Alletson had not yet made an arrest.

" Don't be so harsh, superintendent. My journey may
not have been altogether a waste of time."

" And what might you mean by that?"

" I picked up some information in Venezuela that
could be a lead."

Alletson raised his eye to the ceiling as though pray-
ing for divine guidance. " Amateur detectives. That's all
I need to make my day."

" Don't you want to hear what I discovered? If you
don't I won't trouble you."

" Get on with it," Alletson said. " I'm listening."

" Harry Banner spent some time in a place called
San Borja, which is a one-horse town deep in the heart
of Venezuela. He went to work for a man named Gomara
on an estate about ten miles out of town. Gomara is
now deceased."

" What's all that got to do with this case?"

" Listen," Cade said. " Two men came to San Borja
with Banner. South Americans, probably from Argentina."

" Did they have names?" Alletson allowed himself to
show a small amount of grudging interest.

" Manuel Lopez and Luis Guzman."

Alletson made a note on a pad. " And then?"

" And then Banner suddenly left Gomara's place. He
left San Borja too—in quite a hurry. From all accounts
Lopez and Guzman were mad as hell when they found

he'd gone. They went after him hot-foot."

"And what do you deduce from that, Sexton Blake?" Alletson was mildly sarcastic.

"It seems reasonably obvious. Harry Banner and the other two were in some kind of racket together, perhaps involving this man Gomara. He pulled a fast one on his partners and they went after him. They caught up with him in London and killed him."

"You have been busy," Alletson said. "Did you find out what the racket was?"

"You can't expect me to do all your work," Cade said. "After all, I'm only an amateur detective."

Alletson seemed inclined to make a sharp retort to that, but apparently decided it was not worth his while to bandy words with so unimportant a person.

"I have the descriptions of the two South Americans," Cade said. "Guzman is thin and hard-faced. He wears a drooping moustache and has a small scar on his forehead. Lopez is shorter, thick-set, pockmarked, wearing a gold signet ring."

Alletson's eyes narrowed slightly. "I seem to have heard the second description somewhere before. It sounds very much like the man who tailed you."

"That's what I thought," Cade said.

"The question is why?"

"Why what?"

"Why he tailed you."

"Could be because I was Harry Banner's friend."

"That's hardly a good reason. Or are you suggesting that Lopez and Guzman are going round knocking off all Banner's friends out of revenge for what he did to them?"

" I don't think that's likely."

" Neither do I, Mr. Cade. Do you know what I think?"

" No. Tell me."

" I think you're not coming clean. I think you're not coming entirely clean. I have a nasty little idea at the back of my mind that you're withholding some rather vital information."

Cade looked innocent. " You know me, superintendent. I would never do a thing like that."

" I hope not," Alletson said. " I sincerely hope not. It's an offence, you know. Now, Mr. Cade, I want you to tell me again all that happened on the evening when Mr. Banner came to see you."

" I've told you."

" You may remember something you forgot to mention on the previous occasion. Some little detail that slipped your memory first time round. Just go through it all very carefully from the moment when Banner rang you up."

Cade went through it all very carefully.

" That's the same as before," Alletson said. He sounded a shade disgruntled.

" That's the way it happened. Is that all you want from me?"

" It seems all I'm likely to get."

" I'll be on my way then. You've got my phone number in case you need to get in touch?"

" I've got it," Alletson said.

Cade got up and walked to the door. He said : " You wouldn't like to give me police protection, I suppose?"

" Why should you need police protection?"

" Lopez and Guzman could still be after me."

" If they're still in London."

" I'd say they are."

" I can't give you police protection," Alletson said. " We're short-handed."

" If I'm murdered my blood will be on your head."

" I'll try to bear it with fortitude," Alletson said.

After leaving Alletson Cade made his way to a public house called the Sitting Duck, situated not far from Fenchurch Street Station. It was one of those hostelries that have changed very little since Victorian times, full of mirror glass and mahogany and marble-topped tables with wrought-iron legs. The landlord was an ex-pugilist named Barney Logan and the pub was much frequented by others of that fraternity. The photographs of many past champions adorned the walls, and a pair of boxing-gloves hung symbolically behind the bar, inscribed with the date when Barney Logan had exchanged the ring for the less energetic profession of publican.

It was just a little before one when Cade called in at the public bar, and business looked meagre. There were two old women drinking stout at a table in one corner, a couple of men in the uniform of British Rail disposing of pints of bitter, and a seedy gentleman who was making a small whisky go a very long way indeed.

Barney Logan himself was polishing a glass and looking bored. He had the kind of face that could only have belonged to an ex-pug, all beaten-up and squashed-in and scarred, like something that had been inadvertently allowed to fall into a cement-mixer. When he saw Cade his eye brightened.

" Why, Mr. Cade. Nice to see you. Been a long time."

" Been out of the country," Cade said.

Barney looked envious. " You get around. Me, I don't get around no more. Did once. You ever hear about that fight I had in Chicago?"

" I believe so," Cade said. Everybody who had ever stepped across the threshold of the Sitting Duck had heard about Barney's fight in Chicago. It had been the high-light of his career.

" What's it to be then, Mr. Cade?"

" Scotch from the old square bottle. A large one."

Barney got the drink and accepted Cade's offer of one for himself.

" Good fighting, Mr. Cade."

" Good fighting, Barney."

They drank to that.

" Seen Percy around lately?" Cade asked.

Barney glanced at the clock behind him. " Another ten minutes and he'll be walking through that doorway. You want to see him?"

" I'd like to have a talk with him."

He was on his second whisky when Percy walked in. Percy Proctor had been a middleweight; he had in fact been a very good middleweight. He would probably have had difficulty now in getting down to the eleven stone mark but there was still not a lot of surplus flesh on him. He looked hard, and his face was not beaten-up like Barney's; Percy had been more skilful. He had once done a bit of wrestling too, but he seldom talked about that; he was rather ashamed of it.

" Hallo, Percy," Cade said. " I was looking for you."

" You were?" Percy said. He had a snuffling intonation that came from getting too much leather on the nose. "You wanter write some more about me?"

Cade had once done a feature on Percy for a magazine and had got to know him very well.

" Not this time."

Percy looked disappointed. "I liked that piece you done las' time. Classy, that's what it was, classy. There was words in that there piece I never knew came in the English language."

" I'm glad you liked it. This time I want you to do me a small favour."

" Any time, Mr. Cade, any time. Jus' you say the word an' it's as good as done."

" What'll you have, Percy?"

" I'll have a dirty big pint an' a glass of rum, seein' as you're payin'," Percy said.

Cade gave the order and steered Percy to a corner table. " Now," he said, " this is the set-up."

Cade went up in the lift; it had been repaired during his absence in South America. He got out at the third floor and walked to the door of his flat. He opened the door and went in, and there was that odour of cigar smoke again, the odour he had smelt that day when he had come back from the hotel where Harry Banner's dead body was lying.

If he had been quick enough he might have drawn back, but the men were quicker. One of them seized his arm and pulled him in; the other slipped between him and the door, closing it softly and slipping the catch. The one who had pulled him in was thick-set, pockmarked, wearing a gold signet ring; the other man was thin, hard-faced, with a scar on his forehead above the left eyebrow.

"Manuel Lopez and Luis Guzman," Cade said.

Guzman was holding a flick-knife in his right hand. The blade was clean and shining, but it could have had blood on it not so very long ago—Harry's blood. Blood could be cleaned off.

"We will go in here," Lopez said. "And then we will talk."

He led the way into the sitting-room. Cade followed. With Guzman's knife pricking him in the back, he had no alternative. It made him remember José Rivera, but not with any pleasure.

"Do not shout or do anything else foolish," Guzman said. "Not if you wish to live," He had a harsh, growling voice, and he spoke English with an American intonation.

"I wish to live," Cade said.

"Good. Then do not try any funny business."

"I don't know any funny business," Cade said. "I leave that to the TV comics."

Guzman scowled. Lopez brought up a kitchen chair.

"Sit down," Lopez said.

Cade sat down. Guzman stood on his left and Lopez on his right.

"Now," Lopez said, "you will tell us where they are." His voice was lighter than Guzman's but it had the same American intonation. It had the same menace too.

Cade looked at him with utter innocence. "Tell you where what are?"

"Do not pretend ignorance. We know that Harry

Banner visited you the day he died. We know he left them in your hands."

"Ah," Cade said. "So it was you who searched the flat and threw things about?"

"Yes, we did search."

"And did you find anything?"

"You know we found nothing," Guzman snarled. "Don't act so goddam dumb."

"Then you must know Harry left nothing with me."

"We know he did."

"Did he tell you that before you killed him?"

Guzman pressed the point of the flick-knife into his side and reminded him even more of José. "Perhaps we kill you too, you goddam lousy English bastard."

Lopez cut in sharply : "Wait, Luis. Remember last time."

Cade felt the point move away from his side. He guessed that Lopez was reminding Guzman that they had been too hasty with Banner and that it had better not happen again.

"Take off your coat," Lopez said.

Cade was wearing a raincoat. He stood up and took it off. Lopez snatched it and searched rapidly through the pockets, then threw it aside. He frisked Cade quickly but thoroughly.

"Sit down," he said.

Cade sat down again.

"Do you mind telling me what you're looking for?" he asked.

Lopez said evenly : "You know perfectly well what we are looking for. We are looking for the diamonds that Harry Banner left with you."

"So they were diamonds, were they? Well, think of that. Harry Banner with diamonds. I wonder where he picked them up."

"Never mind where he picked them up. You tell us where you put them."

"I'm sorry," Cade said. "I never had them."

"I better get to work on him," Guzman said. "I make him talk. I make him talk good."

Lopez nodded. "Okay, but careful. Another dead man on our hands is no use at all."

"Trust me," Guzman said.

He put out his left hand and wrenched Cade's jacket open. He tore the shirt open also, baring the skin of Cade's chest and stomach. He stood squarely in front of Cade and rested the point of the flick-knife delicately on the skin just an inch or so above the navel.

"Now tell us," Lopez whispered.

"There's nothing to tell," Cade said.

Guzman put just the smallest pressure on the knife. It was like the prick of a needle.

"Now tell us," Lopez said again.

Cade just looked at him. He was listening, but not to Lopez.

The pressure on the knife increased a little. A trickle of blood like a scarlet thread ran down Cade's stomach.

"It will go in a long way without being fatal," Lopez said. "But it will hurt. Now will you tell us?"

And then Cade heard the sound he had been waiting for; a very small sound; the merest click as of a key turning in a lock perhaps.

"No," he said, "I will not tell you."

He pressed his heels on the floor and tilted the chair

backwards, and as he went over he brought his right foot up hard under Guzman's crotch. Guzman gave a yell of agony and staggered back, dropping the knife and clutching himself.

Lopez acted swiftly. He snatched up the knife and sprang at Cade. And that was when Percy Proctor walked in.

Percy's left hook had always been one of his best punches; it had put better men than Manuel Lopez to sleep. Percy's fist travelled no more than six inches and it took Lopez neatly on the point of the jaw. Lopez went down, out cold.

Guzman was hardly worthy of Percy's attention, but he attended to him nevertheless. As a small favour.

" Is that all, Mr. Cade?"

Cade got up and dabbed his stomach with a handkerchief. Then he buttoned his shirt. " That's all, Percy. And thanks."

" It was hardly worth coming for."

" I began to think you weren't coming. What kept you?"

" That lift," Percy said. " I pressed the button but it never came. In the end I decided to walk."

" Hell," Cade said. " It's broken down again."

Percy held out a key. " You'd better have this back now, Mr. Cade."

Cade took it. " I'll be having that lock changed anyway. People get in too easily. Have you got the cord?"

Percy hauled a length of sash-cord out of his pocket. " All here."

" If you'll just tie them up," Cade said, " I'll ring the

superintendent and tell him to come round and collect. After that we'll have a drink."

" I could do with a drink," Percy said.

FIFTEEN

SOME BUSINESS WITH ARILLA

CADE RANG up Holden Bales before Bales went to work.

" About those small items of merchandise I left in your keeping, Holden."

" Yes?" Bales said.

" I'd like to take them off your hands."

" Can't be too soon for me."

" When shall I come round?"

" This morning. Eleven o'clock. That all right?"

" Okay. Have a good breakfast."

" I've had it," Bales said. " It was lousy. Just between you and me, Bob," he said, lowering his voice, " Ethel is the lousiest cook going."

" I know," Cade said. " I've had meals with you."

Cade walked up the two flights of stairs to Holden Bales's workshop, tapped on the door and pushed it open. The usual mysterious work was going on at the benches and it all looked so dingy that you could hardly imagine that this was the kind of place from which those glittering items of jewellery came. Cade wondered just how much the craftsmen got for their labours, but he knew that it would be useless to ask Holden, because Holden was not the man to give away secrets of that sort.

Nobody appeared to be at all interested in Cade, so he walked across to the door of Bales's tiny office. The door opened just as he got there and revealed Bales himself, unshaven, sandy fringe of hair as unkempt as ever, standing in the opening.

" Ah, there you are, Bob. Began to think you'd forgotten the appointment."

" I'm not late," Cade said.

" Aren't you? That's a change. Come in."

Cade went in. Bales closed the door.

" I'm glad to see you're still at liberty, Bob."

" Why shouldn't I be at liberty?"

" The police might have nabbed you."

" The police haven't got anything on me."

" Haven't they? No, I suppose not. You had the good sense to leave it in my hands, didn't you?"

" Now look here, Holden, if you think—"

Bales lifted his hands in protest. " No, no, I don't think anything. And I don't want to know anything either." He went to the safe, opened it and took out the chamois leather bag. He handed the bag to Cade. " There you are."

" I think I'll just have a look at them," Cade said.

" Don't you trust me?"

" Of course I trust you, Holden. Would I have left them with you if I hadn't? I just want to see if they still look the same."

He unfastened the bag and tipped the diamonds on to

the table. Now that he knew how Harry Banner had come by them they seemed to have acquired a new interest. Those glittering stones had a lot to answer for; they had been the cause of much evil. And yet the stones were not responsible; they were neutral, just so many pieces of hard, bright carbon. It was man, who set so high a value on them, who was responsible; man with his desires, his greed, his cruelty.

" What are you thinking about?" Bales asked.

" Four corpses," Cade said.

" You do have pleasant thoughts. What are you going to do with the diamonds?"

" I thought you didn't want to know anything."

" I don't," Bales said, but Cade could see that he was curious despite himself.

" I'm going to make someone very happy," Cade said.

Bales looked shocked. "Not a woman! Oh dear, I knew you'd make a fool of yourself."

" Holden," Cade said, " you don't know what you're talking about."

He scooped up the diamonds, put them back in the chamois leather bag and dropped the bag into his pocket.

" For God's sake," Bales said, " don't get into trouble. I'd never hear the last of it from Ethel."

" What in hell has it got to do with Ethel?"

" Nothing. She just holds you up as a dreadful example."

" Well, bully for Ethel," Cade said, and he left Bales tugging at the remains of his sandy hair.

It was probably the way Harry Banner had brought them into the country—in his pocket; just walking through the customs as innocently as a new-born babe without the bat of an eyelid. Cade wondered what the air hostesses on the flight down to Argentina would have thought if they had known that he was carrying one hundred and forty thousand pounds' worth of diamonds on his person.

But perhaps it would not have surprised them. Air hostesses saw just about everything; they were probably completely shock-proof.

The flight took him down via Madrid and Lisbon and Bathurst, Recife and Rio. He hated air travel; it made him feel dirty and bleary-eyed and slightly queasy in the stomach. It was one of the questionable blessings of the technological age, and it was so utterly boring. But it did get you where you wanted to be in the shortest possible space of time. And Cade wanted to be in Buenos Aires.

"Will passengers please fasten their seat-belts and refrain from smoking. We are about to land."

Cade fastened his seat-belt and refrained from smoking. He looked out of the window and could see the Rio de la Plata, that broad river on which had once floated the silver from the mines of Alto Peru; he could see too the dock area where now the giant refrigericos, the meat storehouses, stood along the waterfront. Buenos Aires was one of Cade's favourite cities; in Buenos Aires there was never any feeling of being cramped, shut in; it seemed to have borrowed some of the spaciousness of the pampas and to have translated it into urban terms. True, its peace was marred now and then by outbursts of violence, tanks in the streets and armoured cars in the parks and squares; but these were transient phenomena, and after their passing life went on much as before : the trees came into leaf along the Avenida Maipu and roses bloomed in Palermo Park; lovers strolled in the Plaza Mayo and gazed into the shops on the Calle Corrientes; policemen blew their whistles and the sound of ships' sirens came up from the harbour.

And now in Buenos Aires it was spring.

The airliner landed in brilliant sunshine. Cade went through the customs with no trouble at all; he was not asked to turn out his pockets and even his luggage was given only the most cursory of examinations. If it had not been for that faintly unpleasant sense of disorientation that was one of the curses of air travel everything in the garden would have been lovely.

But he forgot about the disorientation when he saw Juanita. She was wearing another of those flowered silk dresses that suited her so well, and an enormous hat with a floppy brim and one red flower as decoration. She did not see him at first, and he just stood looking at her, thinking how beautiful she was and what a splendid figure she had, and wondering why every man in sight did not stop and gaze at her as he was doing, but knowing that he would have resented it if they had.

Then she turned and saw him. She smiled and came towards him, and he went to meet her.

" Roberto."

That she was glad to see him there could be no doubt. It made him glad too. It made the whole boring journey infinitely worth while.

" So you got my cable," he said.

" Yes, Roberto."

" I'm glad you could come."

"Nothing would have prevented me."

He could feel the weight of the diamonds in his pocket. She did not know about them. Later she would know. He hoped the knowledge would make her happy.

"I have a car," she said. "Shall we go?"

"Yes, let's go."

It was a white Jaguar about a year old. She drove expertly. Cade sat beside her and relaxed, content to gaze at the passing panorama of Buenos Aires, even more content to gaze at the profile of Juanita Suarez.

"How was the flight?" she asked.

"Filthy. As always."

"You do not like flying?"

"I endure it. It's useful because it gets you from point A to point B very quickly. That bit in between is best forgotten."

He had reserved a room at a hotel in the Calle San Martin. It was not one of the top class places, but adequate for the proposed term of his stay. He was not yet certain how long that term would be. To some extent it depended on Juanita.

"What are your plans, Roberto?"

"First a shave and a bath. Then perhaps we could have lunch somewhere if that would suit you."

"I would love it."

"Then perhaps a look at Buenos Aires. It's years since I was last here, you know."

"You wish for a guide, señor?"

"I was hoping you would offer."

She dropped him at the hotel.

"I'll be back in an hour. I have some shopping to do."

"Fine," Cade said. He watched her drive away in the direction of the Plaza Mayo.

He went into the hotel and checked in at the reception desk. A bell-boy in blue livery and a lot of brass buttons conducted him to his room. It was on the third floor with a view of the Calle San Martin from the window and a private bathroom.

Cade asked the bell-boy to fetch a sheet of wrapping-paper and a roll of adhesive tape. In scarcely a minute he was back with the required materials. Cade tipped him generously and was rewarded with a grin and a "Gracias, señor."

When the bell-boy had gone Cade wrapped the bag of diamonds in the paper and sealed the parcel with adhesive tape. Then he shaved, had a shower, put on a clean shirt and felt more like a human being.

He wrote his name on the parcel, took it down to the reception desk and asked the clerk to put it in the hotel safe.

"Certainly, señor."

The clerk wrote out a receipt slip and took the parcel to an inner office. He left the door open and Cade could see him twisting the dial of a massive safe. He watched until the clerk had put the parcel away and had re-locked the safe, then left the desk.

"What are your plans for tomorrow?" Juanita asked, looking at him across the glass of burgundy in her hand.

They were dining at a restaurant on the Calle Reconquista. They had had quite a busy day looking at Buenos Aires. They had been to the Zoological Gardens and the Botanical Gardens; they had looked at the Obelisk and the monuments to Christopher Columbus and Admiral Brown, that Irish founder of the Argentine Navy; they had strolled along the Avenida de Mayo from Government House to Congress Hall, the famous Casa Rosada; they had sipped long, cool drinks and watched the world go by. Life could be very pleasant when one was idle and need not think of the necessity of earning a living.

But tomorrow was another day.

" Tomorrow I have to see a man named Arilla."

" Business?"

" Yes, business."

" Where does he live?"

" Oh, way out in the suburbs. Nearly ten miles out."

" You would like me to drive you there?"

" I'd like it very much," Cade said. " I was going to ask you. I want you to be present when I talk to him."

She looked surprised. " For what reason? Does what you are going to talk about concern me?"

" I think it does."

She puckered her forehead. " I cannot think what business you have to discuss with a man named Arilla that could possibly concern me, Roberto."

" Tomorrow you will find out."

" So. You wish to be mysterious."

" Only a small mystery," Cade said. " By weight."

He reclaimed his parcel in the morning and slipped it into his pocket.

" I trust everything is to your satisfaction, Señor Cade," the clerk said.

" Everything," Cade said. He saw Juanita walk into the lobby and repeated under his breath, " Everything."

"Good morning, Juanita."

"Your car is ready, señor."

They walked out of the hotel and got into the white Jaguar.

"To the house of Señor Arilla," Juanita said.

The Jaguar moved smoothly away from the kerb and fitted itself into the stream of traffic.

The house of Señor Alonzo Arilla was a large building that looked rather like a school. It was square, architecturally rather plain, built of brick; it stood in fairly extensive grounds dotted with clumps of trees, very green, very English in appearance. It was in fact an orphanage.

Arilla himself received them in his study. He was a man of about forty, short but vigorous, with crisp black hair and bright, restless eyes. Even when still he seemed to give the impression of superabundant energy; one felt that at any moment he might spring up and dash away on some errand that had just occurred to him.

He welcomed Cade with enthusiasm. "Roberto! How good it is to see you again. It must be at least six years. Much too long."

Cade introduced Juanita. Arilla was delighted to see her. He ushered them both to chairs upholstered in soft red leather, rather worn.

"And what have you been doing since I last saw you?"

"Working," Cade said.

"A regrettable necessity."

It was a large room with two tall windows looking out on to a lawn. On the lawn some children were playing under the supervision of a middle-aged woman.

The sound of their laughter came in through the open windows.

"You still have as many children here?" Cade asked.

Arilla seemed to bounce in his chair. "More. We have no room, but we take them. What else can one do? Turn them away? Tell them to sleep in the streets?"

"You have a soft heart, Alonzo."

Arilla looked fierce. "No, Roberto, I have a very hard heart. It is so hard that I would kill with my own hands anyone I found ill-treating a child. That is the kind of man I am. A villain."

Cade laughed. Juanita laughed too. It would have been difficult to imagine a less villainous man.

Cade stopped laughing. He said : "Now let us get down to business."

Arilla looked surprised. "Business? What business?"

Cade watched the children on the lawn; they were engaged in some intricate game that was a complete mystery to him.

"You spoke to me once about your wish to build a swimming-pool. Have you ever done so?"

Arilla smiled wryly. "Difficult enough to manage on the income we have without such projects."

"Yet you would still like to have a pool?"

"Of course. But why talk of impossibilities?"

"Is it so impossible?"

"Without money, yes. And where would the money come from?"

"Some rich man perhaps."

"Show me the rich man who would give so generously."